The summer of 1945 is both the beginning and end of many things for Ellis Carpenter. Ellis, who's somewhere between being a girl and an adult in these last months of World War II, finds herself struggling with her feelings about both the good things and the bad things that happen that year.

A long war is nearly over—all the more reason to celebrate the coming Fourth of July as never before. But Les McConagy, the soldier–hero of Wissining, Pennsylvania, and a special person to Ellis, is reported missing in action, so how can anyone really have fun?

So much did happen that year—or perhaps it just seems that way to Ellis. But somehow she manages to survive everything from the results of the Citizenship Award Contest to a death dare on the rafters of Sibby's father's barn. And when her best friends, Jules and Sam, go to a dance with her but act different around the girls who wear sweet-smelling cologne and fancy dresses and who lets boys dance close, Ellis survives that, too!

As Ellis' courage and maturity are put to the test, she learns to lock away her love and memories of things ended as a way of opening up more love for beginnings. *Don't Sit Under the Apple Tree* is a nostalgic and moving story which will say many different things to many readers.

Don't Sit Under the Apple Tree

ROBIN F. BRANCATO

Alfred A. Knopf   New York

THIS IS A BORZOI BOOK PUBLISHED BY ALFRED A. KNOPF, INC.

Copyright © 1975 by Robin F. Brancato. All rights reserved under International and Pan-American Copyright Conventions. Published in the United States by Alfred A. Knopf, Inc., New York, and simultaneously in Canada by Random House of Canada Limited, Toronto. Distributed by Random House, Inc., New York. Manufactured in the United States of America.

LIBRARY OF CONGRESS CATALOGING IN PUBLICATION DATA

Brancato, Robin F. Don't sit under the apple tree.   Summary: A young girl living in a small Pennsylvania town relates her and her friends activities in and out of school during the last months of World War II. [1. World War, 1939–1945—United States—Fiction] I. Title. PZ7.B73587DO [Fic] 74-15305 ISBN 0-394-83034-2 ISBN 0-394-93034-7 (lib. bdg.) 0 9 8 7 6 5 4 3 2 1

For John, Chris and Greg

Don't Sit Under
the Apple Tree

One

"Hey, Ellis! Hey—Ellie-Belly," Sam shouted, "you can't *prove* Hitler's dead!"

"He *is*," I said. "It was in the newspapers!" Sam might be right, though, I had to admit. Some people were saying that maybe Hitler, the German dictator, had gotten away.

The weather was clearing as we walked to school past the wide lawns of the Barth mansion and on toward the playground. There was something special in the air— maybe it was the excitement of V-E Day, or maybe it was just the perfume of lilac bushes. The morning rain had washed earthworms onto the sidewalk and I walked on tiptoe so I wouldn't step on any.

"Hey, Ellis!" Sam cried. Jumping out from behind a hedge, he picked up an earthworm and dangled it in my direction. "Ellis," he snorted, "where'd you get your dumb name, anyway? That's no girl's name!"

"I got it from Miss Mary Ellis," I said. "She was a good friend of my family, and my grandmother says Mary Ellis was a courageous person."

"They gave her name to the wrong kid, then," Sam

laughed. He danced along next to me, waving the earthworm in my face. Sam Goff was a pain. The gang of us from Milford Square—Sam and Jules and the little kids and I—always walked to school together, but sometimes I wished Sam the Monkeyface would get lost.

"Spit, spit, right in the Führer's face!" Sam was yelling. He ran beside us and sent spit flying as close to Jules and me as he could come without hitting us.

"Hitler's dead, stupid," I said. "It's V-E Day, Victory in Europe—the Nazis surrendered yesterday," I told him. "Miss Fenster says May 7, 1945, will go down in history. If you don't stop it we'll be late for school, and Miss Fenster won't let us hear the announcement on the radio!"

I took a step toward him and gave Sam a sudden push into the hedges that wound around the lawn of the Barths, the richest people in Wissining.

"Ow! I'll get you for that, Ellis Carpenter!" Sam yelled. I dodged him and looked for help from Jules. But Jules McConagy, my best friend, was walking along not paying the least bit of attention to Sam and me. And that didn't surprise me. In the last month or so Jules had gotten very quiet, ever since the telegram had come about his brother Les. Les McConagy had gone off to war. The telegram from the War Department had said that Les was missing in action.

"Maybe Hitler escaped and came in a submarine to America," Sam said, not letting up. His eyes narrowed. "Maybe he's going to hide out here until he can start another war." Sam was always looking for ways to get everybody scared and angry. I tried to understand him as much as I could because his mother had died when he was born. His stepmother was pretty nice, but she was away a lot, working at her job to help the war effort. Still, it was pretty hard to put up with him.

"Hitler's going to hide out with your grandmother," Sam said. "She'll let him, because she's a *German*."

"She used to be a German," I said. "She's American now." I ran ahead, partly to get away from Sam and partly because I didn't want to be late. Miss Fenster was going to tune in President Harry S Truman on the radio, and we were going to paste more pictures in our World War II scrapbook.

"Your grandmother was born in Germany, wasn't she?" Sam asked. He took long leaps to catch up with me.

"Yes." It bothered me to admit it, but I had to.

"Well, if you're born in Germany you're a German!" Sam shouted in my ear. "And if you're related to her *you're* a Nazi too!"

"You're crazy!" I told him. "I'm an American, and if a person lives here long enough they become an American." I was pretty sure about that. My Grossie— that was the nickname my little brother Mick and I used for our *Grossmutter,* or grandmother—had come to America from Germany when she was sixteen. Of all the people in the world, my Grossie was the last one I could picture walking with a goose step, and saluting and shouting "Heil, Hitler!" like the Germans in the movies.

"Germans all love Hitler," Sam said, screwing up his face. "You'll wait, she'll hide him!"

I hoped not, but if Hitler ever came around badly wounded or something Grossie might take him in, I thought, just because she was so kind. Still, I couldn't believe Grossie *liked* Hitler. Probably she had left Germany just to get away from him.

"Hitler's dead," I said again uncertainly. Our teacher Miss Fenster was always showing us gory newspaper photographs of dead war criminals hanging upside down, but so far there weren't any such pictures of Hitler.

All of a sudden Jules stepped quietly between Sam and me. "V-E Day is the best day of my life so far," he said out of the blue as if he hadn't heard one word about Hitler. His face looked serious as usual. Jules' straight reddish blond hair hung down to his eyes. He wore glasses, and even though glasses made some kids look like dopes, they made Jules look good.

"This is your best day?" I was surprised. My best days were Christmas and the Fourth of July.

"My best day *so far,*" he repeated. "The very best will be the day Les comes back."

I nodded. That would be my best day too. Everybody on Milford Square loved Jules' big brother Les. All the kids looked up to him, especially me. When I was little I often used to sit in our rose arbor, and if Les came by he would stop and look up at me and say, "Hi, Ellis, Ellis, sitting on the trellis!"

Before he had gone off to war I used to lie in bed at

night and pretend that Les was my older brother. And when he went away on the very next day after high school graduation I clipped his picture out of the newspaper, pasted it in a notebook and started to write a story about him. I used to add a little bit to the story of Les every night until we heard that he was missing in action. Then I stopped. I was afraid to write the ending.

Sam finally let off teasing me as the three of us walked side by side. Probably he felt ashamed when he heard us talking about Les. Even Sam admired Les McConagy.

"Do you think your brother'll ever come back?" Sam asked Jules. Sam always asked about personal things that other people were too polite to mention.

Jules nodded.

"How do you think you'll find out that he's alive?" Sam went on. "Will your mother get another telegram?"

Jules looked straight ahead. "I just have a feeling he'll come back," he said.

In the school yard I waited up for my brother Mick, to make sure he was all together. He and Sam's half sister Ruthie were always tagging behind the rest of us. Ruthie's underpants were showing as usual, so I gave them a tug before we went along into school.

By the time I got inside Miss Fenster's room the day had turned out to be sunny. It was warm enough to open the windows at the top with a long window pole. I stood looking out over the school yard and beyond, past the playground, to where Wissining Creek wound through the woods. Wissining is a little town on the outskirts of Windsor, Pennsylvania. A lot of Pennsylvania Dutch—really Pennsylvania Germans—had settled here, but most people thought of themselves as just plain Americans. There were some very rich people like the Barths, and some medium rich like the Lanes, but most were average.

"Come, boys and girls, gather around my desk," Miss Fenster said when the late bell rang. "History is in the making!" If history was in the making as often as she said it was, our social studies books would have weighed a ton. The things Miss Fenster loved the most were stories about American prisoners of war who survived in jungles and about women spies like one named Tokyo Rose. Miss Fenster was really in her glory because it was V-E Day. I wondered what she would do with herself after the war was over and there were no more war bulletins on the radio and no more sickening clippings for us to paste in the class scrapbook.

Miss Fenster fiddled around with the dial of the radio she had brought from home. When she found the right station we all pressed our ears as close as we could to hear the voice of President Harry S Truman. Half the war was over, Truman said.

When the broadcast ended Miss Fenster motioned for us to bow our heads in silence. "Let's pray for the capture of Emperor Hirohito," she said, "so that we will have peace at last." At the end of one minute she raised her head.

"There are two very important items of business for

us to take care of today," she said. "First, we have a special activity for tomorrow. As you know, there is still much more work to do for the war. And luckily for us the mother of someone in this class has made a very generous offer." We all looked at each other. Miss Fenster went on, "Mrs. Lane has invited the whole class to the Lane farm tomorrow to gather milkweed pods for the war effort."

Sibby Lane beamed until I thought her face would crack. She annoyed me. Her nose was always running, and she tried too hard to be friends. Sibby the Simp, we called her.

"We'll leave for the farm at ten o'clock tomorrow," said Miss Fenster. "Mr. Lane will send his truck to transport us." Everybody cheered. That meant all twenty of us would be piling into the truck for the trip out to the farm. The Lanes must have been pretty rich. Mr. Lane wasn't really a farmer—he had a big business in Windsor and owned the truck and the barn and the farmhouse just for fun. The Lane's farm was a wonderful place. I had been invited there lots of times because Sibby the Simp was always trying to get me to be her best friend.

"Everyone is to bring lunch," said Miss Fenster. "The purpose of the trip will be to look for milkweed and to collect the pods in sacks for the soldiers."

"Soldiers eat *that?*" Sam asked.

"Of course not," Miss Fenster sighed. "The fluffy insides of the pods are used for filling soldiers' life jackets. Things are scarce during a war. We must make use of whatever we can." The whole class started buzzing about the trip.

"Quickly now, boys and girls," Miss Fenster held up her hand to stop the racket. "Our second item of business is even more important. Each year at this time we nominate a student from this grade for the annual Citizenship Award. The winner will be announced at our end-of-the-year ceremonies."

Suddenly I got a funny feeling. I was in the oldest class—the leaders of the school. The Citizenship Award was the biggest honor there was. Les McConagy had won it when he was in our grade.

"I nominate myself!" Sam called out.

Miss Fenster shook her head sadly. "All of you have a responsibility," she said, looking at Sam. "If we should choose the wrong person, we will be letting our country down." She picked up a piece of chalk and stood by the blackboard. "Are there any nominations?"

When I saw Sibby Lane's hand go up I knew what it meant for sure.

"Sybil?"

"I nominate Ellis Carpenter," Sibby said. Sibby always hung around me and nominated me for things. Miss Fenster wrote my name on the board. Then John Elting nominated his best friend, Bruce Brown, and somebody else nominated John Elting.

When Miss Fenster turned around one hand was still up. Philip Helmuth, who loved girls, had his arm stretched out so that he was just about touching Sally's hair.

Philip stood up. "I nominate Sally Cabeen," he said. I knew Sally would get nominated. She was prettiest in the class, and her father was a major in the Army. When she heard her name Sally tossed her blond hair and smiled at Philip. Philip Helmuth was okay, but I preferred boys like Jules who didn't love girls.

"Any more nominations?" asked Miss Fenster, but there was no chance to answer because at that moment bells started ringing. Bells rang everywhere! The school bell clanged and church bells sounded outside. Miss Fenster looked at us in openmouthed surprise. "Oh, my stars!" she said.

There was a knock at the door. Miss Fenster opened it, and we could see her standing in the hallway talking to Mrs. Rice, the principal.

"Good news, boys and girls," Miss Fenster said to us, when Mrs. Rice had waved and walked away. "In honor of V-E Day, school is dismissed early!" Everyone shouted and whistled. "Now, now," Miss Fenster reminded us, putting up her hand for silence, "remember your lunches tomorrow, and remember your manners—we're going to the Lane's farm!"

Two

It was so crowded in the truck the next morning that I thought we weren't all going to be allowed to ride together on the trip to the farm. Mrs. Lane finally agreed that we could all pile in, if we promised not to make noise. Mrs. Lane and Miss Fenster led the way in Lane's old station wagon. Some of us stood and some of us sat on the floor of the truck as we bounced along on the milkweed expedition. The morning heat made all the lunches blend together, so that the whole inside of the truck ended up smelling like bananas and peanut butter.

Once we got on the open road we forgot our promise to Mrs. Lane, and we sang loud songs like, "Off we go, into the wild, blue yonder," and "Would you like to swing on a star, carry moonbeams home in a jar?" I was squashed between Jules and Philip Helmuth.

"Hey, Jules," I whispered, leaning toward him. There was something I had been wanting to ask him. "What did you mean yesterday when you told Sam you had a 'feeling' Les was safe? What kind of a feeling?"

"Shhhh." Jules gave me a signal. "I'll tell you later," he said.

The minute we got to the Lane's farm Miss Fenster put us to work, as if the faster we pulled milkweed, the sooner Hirohito would be falling on his sword. One of her favorite subjects was hari-kari, the Japanese soldier's method of killing himself with honor. I figured that the day that would really go down in history for Miss Fenster would be the one when Hirohito finally did it.

The milkweed was plentiful. Miss Fenster and Mrs. Lane handed out cloth sacks, and in groups of two or three we worked to fill them with pods. The sun blazed down on the field, and the juice from the stems made us sticky. I held the bag open as Jules, perspiration steaming up his glasses, reached up to pull the pods off the stalks.

"Do you really get silent messages?" I asked Jules when we were all by ourselves.

"Yes, sometimes." He brushed the hair out of his eyes and looked around. "But don't tell anyone."

"What are they about—the messages?" I whispered.

"About what's going to happen," he said. "About whether people are safe or in danger."

"Are the messages always right?" I let the sack fall to the ground.

"Most of the time."

"I wouldn't like it," I said. "Say you got a bad message. You'd know it before it happened, and you'd be sad all that much longer." He nodded as if I were right. "Did you . . ." I looked at Jules with hesitation, "did you ever get a secret message about Les before the telegram came?"

"Yes," he said quietly. "But *don't tell anyone*," he said.

I looked into his eyes. "I swear I won't."

By lunchtime more than thirty sacks of milkweed pods lined the road. Lane's hired man came by in the truck and loaded the pods so that he could take them into Windsor. The field next to the Lane's house was steamy in the heat. A few kids who were always weak and tired flung themselves down in the prickly grass. Phil Helmuth sat close to Sally Cabeen, who giggled every time he tried to whisper something in her ear. Bruce Brown was catching grasshoppers and trying to stuff them down the necks of all the girls when Mrs. Lane called us to the edge of the road.

"What hard workers!" she said. Mrs. Lane was very tall and straight-backed. She looked strong like a pioneer woman, which made me wonder how she happened to have a daughter who was so silly and babyish. "I invite you all to rest now," she said. "Come to the barn where it's cool." Mrs. Lane walked behind with Miss Fenster while we ran to the barn.

"Come on, Jules," I said. "Last one there's a monkey's uncle—Sam's uncle!" I had played in Sibby's barn before, and I wanted to show Jules how to walk on the rafters.

The idea caught on quickly. Bruce hoisted himself up right after me, and soon all but the sissy kids had crawled high up in the rafters and were perched in the air, looking down on blocks of clean, strong-smelling hay that were stacked far below around the edges of the barn. Through the loft window I saw Mrs. Lane and Miss Fenster go into the house. The barn rafters were wooden beams just as wide as a pair of shoes. The only way to move along safely was by gently inching forward with arms stretched out for balance. So long as we moved along the outer edges, there was no danger—the hay would break a fall. Some kids even jumped down into the hay on purpose. But Bruce Brown wasn't satisfied. He had to be a show-off as usual.

"Lookee!" Bruce cried, as he moved along his rafter. "Anybody for the Daredevils' Club, follow me!" Shuffling at top speed, he didn't stop until he was in the very center of the barn. Over his head a ray of sun lighted up a nest of cobwebs. Thirty feet under him lay the cement floor. Everyone down below and everyone on the rafters stopped moving. There was an uneasy murmur.

"Bruce, come down!" Sally pleaded, but he only laughed.

"My father says not to go where there's no hay," Sibby called to him.

"President of the Daredevils' Club!" Bruce shouted. He seemed not to hear. Anyway, he was at a point of no return. Half admiring him and half panicked, I held my breath as I watched Bruce scoot above the cold cement. I looked around for Jules to see if I could read in his face any message about Bruce's danger, but Jules had his back to me.

Two-thirds of the way across the open space, Bruce stopped. "Who's going to follow me?" he shouted.

"John, where are you?" John Elting, smiling weakly, stood on top of the hay, clinging hard to the end of Bruce's rafter. His face was pale.

"John, where are you?" Bruce called again. "You gonna make me turn around and look?"

"Bruce, *please* don't turn around," Sally screamed.

"I'm going to turn around," Bruce threatened, as he moved slightly forward.

"I'll tell my father!" Sibby cried. We all knew her father wasn't home. Suddenly it struck me that the whole thing was my fault. I had started the rafter walking in the first place. How did I know that Bruce would be such a show-off? Still, I was the one who had gotten him into it. If he fell I'd never forgive myself.

"I'm turning around," Bruce teased again in a sing-song voice.

"Wait, Bruce, don't." John had pulled himself up onto the end of the same rafter. Pale and shaking, he inched forward.

"He answered you, Bruce, don't turn around," Sally called.

"I'm coming, Bruce." John's voice sounded strange. Probably even Bruce noticed that. Everyone stood like statues, watching first Bruce with his arms outstretched and then John, who was now just over the point where the hay ended.

"Don't bother," Bruce shouted. "Don't bother coming," and as he said it, he waved his hand in a way that showed he had forgotten where he was. The movement of his hand was just enough to upset his balance. There was a horrible second or two when the eyes of everyone focused on Bruce as he wobbled back and forth. Then, like a person grabbing the back of a train as it pulls out of the station, he took great steps forward, his feet by some miracle touching the rafter, until at a certain point he completely lost his balance. Just over the place where the hay began, he leaped, threw himself forward with a racing dive, and landed with a dull thump on his stomach in the hay.

"Oh, Bruce," Sally sobbed. John let himself down gently from the rafter on the opposite side of the barn. Sam Goff, who was nearest Bruce, put his face near Bruce's.

"Y' okay, Bruce?" Bruce lay still, so that some of the others close by started gathering around him. I held my breath. "Bruce?" Sam repeated. Sam lay his hand on Bruce's shirt. "Bruce?" Then all of a sudden Sam jumped back. Bruce leaped up on both feet like a man shot out of a cannon at a carnival.

"President of the Daredevils' Club!" Bruce shouted, grinning. I laughed along with everybody else, but when it came time to eat lunch I wasn't very hungry.

Miss Fenster joined us while we were eating lunch, and afterward as we cleaned up our leftovers, she said to the whole group, "I'm happy that while I was inside the house I didn't have to worry about loud noise and disturbance from over here in the barn. I'm glad you've all been so mature in your behavior today. Until the truck comes back for us Mrs. Lane says you may play freely in and around the barn. But please don't climb up on the hay," Miss Fenster warned us. "Someone might slip, and others of you might be susceptible to hay fever. And please remember," she whispered out loud, "to say thank you to the Lanes when we leave."

I felt bad. I always felt guilty when someone said we were good and we really weren't. I wanted to tell Miss Fenster about Bruce on the rafters just to be honest, but it would have sounded like tattling. Besides, I didn't want Miss Fenster to have a heart attack. Whenever up-setting things happened she was always saying, "Oh, my heart!"

After Miss Fenster had complimented us, Jules, Sally and a few others headed for the swings in the yard—swings made of old rubber tires suspended from a tree. They must have been very old tires, because you couldn't get rubber at all during the war. I felt like going with them, but just then Sibby asked me if I would come inside the house with her, and I said I would just to see what she wanted.

The house was dark and quiet. The kitchen, looking practically like one in colonial days, had a rag rug on the floor, pots hanging from the walls, and besides the regular stove for cooking, there was an old potbellied stove that people used for keeping warm in the old days. Sibby stopped to blow her nose, as usual. Maybe she had hay fever, I thought.

"What do you want?" I asked her.

"Come with me," she said. "My mother wants to see you." She pulled me through the kitchen and up the stairs toward the second-floor sitting room.

"Wants to see *me*? What for?"

"My mother likes you." I figured she did, since she was always having Sibby invite me, but it didn't make sense that she would want to see just me, when the whole class was running around outside.

Mrs. Lane was standing straight as a board in the sitting room, a cheerful place with flowered chintz curtains and slipcovers.

"Here she is," Sibby said, and before I knew it she had disappeared and left me alone with her mother. I looked at her in confusion.

"Hello, Ellis," she smiled, taking my hands and leading me over to the chintz-covered couch. It was the first time I had ever seen her close up. She had very rosy cheeks, something like a painted wooden doll's. "Have you had a good time today?" she asked.

"Oh, yes," I said.

"You know, Ellis, of all Sibby's friends, *you* are the one I like best."

I felt myself getting flushed in the face.

"Are you aware, Ellis, of how much Sibby admires and respects you?" Mrs. Lane didn't wait for an answer. "You are her favorite friend," she smiled. "Is it true, Ellis," she turned sharply toward me, "that there is an election in class tomorrow for the Citizenship Award?"

"Yes," I said. Mrs. Lane paused and picked her words carefully.

"You were nominated for the award, weren't you?"

"Yes . . ." I couldn't imagine what it had to do with her.

"Who nominated you?"

"Sibby did."

She nodded. "Just as I thought. Sibby often shows her friendship for you, doesn't she?"

"Yes, I guess so." Sibby was always trying to get in good with people.

"Ellis," she put her hand on my arm, "has it ever occurred to you to show *your* friendship for *Sibby?*" What did she mean? I tried to show friendship by coming to her house even though I didn't like to play with her that much.

"I try to be friends . . ." I said.

"Ellis, if you think about how much Sibby likes you and how much *she's* helped *you,* maybe you'll see what I mean." I didn't see anything except her rosy cheeks, which seemed to have become redder since the beginning of our conversation.

"Am I correct that there could be another nomination for the Citizenship Award tomorrow?" she asked.

"I guess so . . ."

"Could you make that nomination?" she whispered. I must have looked like an imbecile. I had thought of nominating Jules, but I knew that wasn't what Mrs. Lane was talking about.

"Who?" I asked.

"Wouldn't it be a good way to show friendship to Sibby if you nominated her for the Citizenship Award?" Mrs. Lane's eyes filled up, almost as if she were going to cry.

"But . . ." I couldn't believe my ears. Mrs. Lane was

telling me to nominate Sibby. "I guess so," I mumbled. It seemed impossible for me to tell somebody's mother, especially Mrs. Lane, "No, I won't do it." Mrs. Lane made it sound as if it were so important to her. Well, maybe it wouldn't hurt me to put up Sibby's name, just to make them both feel good. She would never win—I wouldn't have to worry about that. Still, I felt my face burning, and I wanted to be out of that room more than anything else in the world.

"Then you'll do it?" she asked. My head swam. I couldn't make any words come out. Suddenly, though, the answer hit me like a flash. It was so simple.

"I'd like to, Mrs. Lane," I said with relief, "but I can't. Sibby nominated me, and we aren't allowed to nominate back."

"What do you mean 'back'?"

"I can't put up the person who put me up," I explained. "We have a rule."

"Oh, I see," she said. "Well, there's no reason why you couldn't find someone else to do it, is there? All the children have such respect for you."

"I don't know," I swallowed hard. "I guess I could try."

"Sibby'd appreciate that." Then she added, "And so would I. Remember, Ellis, Sibby doesn't make friends as easily as you do, and you're her best friend."

"I know," I said stupidly. The light had faded in the sitting room, and even Mrs. Lane's cheeks looked paler. She got up and took me by the hand. I didn't feel like touching her, but I had no choice.

"Thank you, dear," she said, leading me to the door. "I'm glad that Sibby has such a good friend. Please come again soon, Ellis." We started down the stairs. "There's the truck now—I see it coming around the bend." At the bottom of the steps she stooped and kissed me on the forehead.

"Good-bye, dear," she said. "I'm so glad we had our little talk, and do remember . . ." As her words trailed off she turned away from me and burst through the kitchen door into the yard. The next minute she was swarmed by everyone who had come to say thank you. I felt strange, as if I had dreamed the conversation with Mrs. Lane.

We got into the truck, and everyone but me waved good-bye to Sibby and her mother until at the end of the road we couldn't see them any longer. On the way home I didn't talk much. I couldn't exactly say why I felt so awful, so embarrassed, except that I knew Mrs. Lane had done something silly. Mrs. Lane was a grown-up, and a grown-up should have known better.

"How was the trip?" my father asked at supper.

"Okay." I still didn't feel like talking.

"Did you eat all kinds of junk?" My mother shot me an accusing look.

"Practically none."

"Then why are you just twiddling with your noodles?"

"Not hungry," I said.

"Why not?" she asked. Suddenly I burst into tears. I

admit it wasn't a very courageous Citizenship Award thing to do, but I couldn't help it.

"For heaven's sake, what is it?" my mother asked. My brother Mick dropped his fork and stared at me.

"Mrs. Lane . . ." I was gasping from the effort of trying not to cry.

"What about her?" My father leaned over and handed me his napkin to catch the tears.

"She's making me . . . nominate Sibby for the Citizenship Award!"

"She can't *make* you, can she?" he asked. I explained what had happened at the Lane's while all three listened.

"That's too bad," my mother said, shaking her head. "Mrs. Lane shouldn't have done that." But I could tell that none of them understood how bad I felt.

"I know what I'll do," I said. "I'll get Jules to nominate her as a favor, but neither of us will vote for her."

"That sounds peculiar to me," said my father. "You'd be forcing Jules just as Mrs. Lane is trying to force you. You'd be doing the same thing she did." I saw that, but I was afraid not to do what Mrs. Lane wanted. She scared me. Then while my parents were thinking quietly, Mickey looked up.

"*Is* Sibby a good citizen?" he asked.

"No!" I burst out, half crying and half laughing. "She's a terrible citizen!" That evening I told myself I would put off deciding what to do until the next day, but Mickey's question had gotten through to me.

Three

When Miss Fenster reminded us in the morning that the Citizenship Award election would be held in the afternoon, I could see that Sibby's eyes were on me. I had avoided looking at her and talking to her. Fortunately we were kept very busy drawing pictures of milkweed pods and writing thank-you notes to Mr. and Mrs. Lane. As we were walking back to school after lunch, I was still debating what to do.

"Jules," I said, "would you do anything I asked you?"

"I wouldn't jump in the middle of the mine hole," he said. The mine hole was a small lake near our house. Everybody claimed that once, while miners were at work, water had suddenly sprung up from the bottom. The miners had run for their lives. The middle was supposed to be very deep and still full of huge machinery.

"Would you do something that was just words—not hurting anybody?"

"Depends. What?"

"Would you nominate somebody if I wanted you to?"

"For what? Who?"

"Sibby for Good Citizen?"

"No." He didn't even have to think about it.

"Why not?"

"Because she's a terrible citizen." It was no use. I knew I wouldn't get anywhere with Jules when he had his mind made up.

"It's time now to complete our unfinished business," said Miss Fenster when the afternoon session started. "At the end of today I must submit the name of the person you elect for the Good Citizenship Award. The teachers and the principal, Mrs. Rice, must also agree on this person. They have a vote too. The award will be presented at the end-of-the-year ceremonies on the evening of June 8, when all your parents will be there.

"Now," she said, "you see the names of our four fine nominees." She had already written my name, Bruce's, John's and Sally's on the board. "Are there any further nominations?"

The room was silent. I could feel Sibby's eyes boring into me. What I really wanted to do was to nominate Jules, but I decided not to. Everyone knew that Jules and I were friends, and they would think I was doing it just for friendship. They might even think I did it because I *loved* Jules, which would be even worse. So I didn't raise my hand.

Miss Fenster cleared her throat. "Am I correct that there are no further nominations?" I could hear Sibby sighing loudly. I pictured her mother's face when she found out that Sibby wasn't on the list, and I moved my arm slightly. Just then Jimmy Henninger's hand went up, and Miss Fenster called on him.

"I move that the nominations be closed." Bruce Brown seconded it, and before I could do anything, the motion was passed.

"I'm glad we have such fine nominees," said Miss Fenster. "James, will you please distribute the ballots?" As the slips of paper were passed back, Sibby raised her hand.

"May I go to the lavatory, Miss Fenster?" Miss Fenster nodded, and Sibby got up. As she walked past me, she purposely stepped on my foot, but I didn't make a sound even though it hurt. I couldn't tell for sure if she was crying, but I think she was.

"Tough luck," I tried to say to myself. But I couldn't stop imagining her mother doing something awful— coming to school maybe, to tell Miss Fenster that I didn't keep my word; or maybe Sibby herself would tell Mrs. Rice, the principal, that I was the one who had started walking on the rafters.

It was hard to concentrate on who to vote for. I never voted for myself; that would be conceited. Second I eliminated Sally, not because all the boys thought she was beautiful, but because she was always trying too hard to get in good with teachers. Next I decided not to vote for Bruce because he was such a show-off. That left John Elting, who was a pretty good citizen. Not as good as Jules, but the best on the list. Sibby came back, we voted and the ballots were collected and Miss Fenster erased the names from the board.

"You'll find out who won," she said, "on the evening of June 8."

"*You* can't get the Citizenship Award," said a voice. I jumped so hard I bumped Jules and knocked him off the curb, as we walked home past the Barth's mansion. Behind the hedge I saw Sam's face. Sam must have planned to run ahead and scare us.

"Who says I can't?"

"I do," Sam said. "You can't get the award because of your grandmother."

"They aren't giving it to her."

"They do a check on everyone," Sam sneered. "If somebody has a relative who hides the enemy—or who *might* hide the enemy—the person's out. No Citizenship Award."

"You're crazy."

"My father said so, and he's an air raid warden." It was true that Sam's father had a metal helmet and came around during air raid drills to make sure the lights were out, but the business about checking up on my grandmother still sounded fishy to me.

"Let's start a club," Jules said. Sometimes when I was sure Jules was listening quietly, he was really off in another world thinking up some idea.

"What club?" I asked.

"Model airplane?" Jules suggested.

"Well . . ." I hesitated. That didn't sound like much of a club to me.

"A war club, us against Tim Feeney!" Sam said.

"No," I told him. Sam always wanted to be against Tim Feeney, who lived on Milford Square but went to St. Agatha's, a Catholic school. "No fighting club," I said. "Let's do good." I admit it. Having my name up for the Citizenship Award had started the old halo glowing and wings sprouting.

"Let's make model airplanes," Jules said, "and sell them, and give magic shows, and use all the money for war bonds."

"Okay," I agreed. "We can make the models out of toothpicks and tissue paper, like Les used to. Meet on my porch," I said. "I'll be president."

Jules looked up. "I suggested the club," he mentioned politely. "Meet in my cellar," Jules said. "*I'll* be president."

The McConagy's cellar was dark and musty in a pleasant, peaceful way. It was filled with more games than any other place I had ever seen. Even though most of the games were from when Les was little, they were all stacked neatly on wooden shelves, and none of the pieces were missing. Most had been in the cellar so long that they carried a cellar smell along with them even when we took them upstairs so we could play by the big radio.

I was the first one at the meeting. "Go get the other kids," Jules whispered. Since the day when the telegram had come saying that Les was missing, we were very careful not to make noise in Jules's house. It was as if news of Les might arrive at any minute, and we wanted to be ready to hear it. Jules spread out white tissue paper and poured out a box of flat toothpicks on the cement floor, while I ran up the cellar steps and out the front door.

"Hey, Mick!" I shouted. "Yo, Ruthie!" Sam and Tim were chasing the two little kids around the grassy mall in the middle of Milford Square. The square was a quiet street shaped like a U, so that everybody lived close to everybody else. Right in the middle of the mall was a sign that said:

KEEP OFF THE GRASS
BY ORDER OF THE WISSINING POLICE DEPT.

"Sam, Tim, come on!" I called. "The club's starting!" But they didn't pay any attention. Sam leaped over the KEEP OFF THE GRASS sign and knocked it flat.

"Sam, get off of there," I warned him. But it was too late. Old Mrs. Lukesh, who lived at the end of the Square, was already out on her front porch. Mrs. Lukesh loved grass. Whenever she saw kids playing on the mall, she dropped whatever she was doing in her creepy house and came out to waggle her finger at us.

"You children!" she called now to Sam and Tim in a shaky voice. "Get off that grass! Get off that grass right this minute, or I'll call the police!"

Sam jumped over the fallen sign a few times, just to get her mad enough so that she would go in to telephone the cops. As soon as she had disappeared inside, Sam, Tim, Mick and Ruthie came running.

"The cops are coming! The cops are coming!" Sam shouted so loudly that Mick and Ruthie ran screaming into the McConagy's house. When I had shushed them we went down to the cellar where Jules was already working on a model airplane.

"That's nice, Jules," I said. Sticking the tiny toothpicks together with glue was hard, and I could tell right away that the little kids weren't going to be any good at making airplanes. "Go to our house and get a flat box to put the planes in," I told Mick, just to get rid of him. "You and Ruthie can carry the box when we go around trying to sell the models."

I wished there were more kids in the neighborhood to join the club and help us make money, but the only person we could have gotten was that sissy Willie Pflug from the next street, and his fingers were too fat to make toothpick airplanes. Sibby would have joined even though she lived far away. Her father's truck probably would have brought her specially. But I didn't feel like putting up with Sibby. I didn't want a simp in our club.

By the time Mick and Ruthie had come back with the carton, Jules, Sam, Tim and I had each finished a model airplane. The tissue paper on Sam's was half hanging off, and mine had blobs of glue all over it, but Jules had made a P-39 that really looked like a plane.

"Let's charge fifty cents for Jules'," I said, "and ten

cents for the others." We let Mick and Ruthie carry the box between them as we went around to the houses of Milford Square.

"Let's go to your house first," Sam said to me.

"No, my mother'll buy one for sure," I told him. "Let's go other places and let them get first pick. My mother'll buy one even if it's crummy."

"No one's home at my house," Sam said. His step-mother worked in a defense plant. She was never home. At the Shoppe's house, next to Sam's, the grown-up daughter admired Jules' plane and bought it right away for fifty cents.

"She must have bought it just to be nice," Jules said, as we walked away. What I liked about Jules was that he never bragged.

"No, it was really good looking," I told him. "She admired it."

After my mother and Mrs. McConagy had each bought a plane, our luck ran out. At the other houses we tried, either nobody was home or nobody wanted to buy the plane that Sam had made.

"Let's float it in the mine hole," Sam suggested.

"No." Jules shook his head. "We'll make one more sale."

"Where?" I couldn't imagine what Jules was think-ing of. He walked ahead of the rest of us with the model airplane in the palm of his hand.

"Hey, Jules, where are you going?" Sam asked. "Jules, you're nuts!" Jules had led us to the end of the Square straight to the door of Mrs. Lukesh, who loved grass.

"I'm leaving!" Sam said. "She'll call the cops!" Mick and Ruthie hid in the bushes.

"Jules," I pleaded. "What does Mrs. Lukesh want with a toy airplane?" He ignored me and knocked sharply on the knocker. Mrs. Lukesh didn't have a doorbell.

"Who's there?" said a feeble voice.

Jules knocked again. The door opened a tiny crack, and a smell like leftover lamb stew seeped out.

"What do you want?" Close up, Mrs. Lukesh was even smaller and skinnier than I remembered.

Jules cleared his throat. "The Milford Square Good Citizens' Model Airplane Club is selling this model airplane to raise money for war bonds. It's our last one. Would you care to buy it? It's only ten cents."

"Heh?" Mrs. Lukesh opened the door a crack wider. Even though Tim and Sam were giggling, Jules repeated his speech and I held out the money we had made to show her.

"No, no. I don't believe so," she croaked, when Jules was finished for the second time. "Don't believe so. Not today," and she shut the door without another word.

"The old crow!" Sam snorted. He pulled a piece of chalk out of his pocket and started drawing a swastika on the front steps, but Jules stopped him.

"She's deaf," Jules said. "Maybe she didn't understand."

"She hears us pretty good when we're playing on the mall," Sam grumbled.

"Let's leave the plane on her step." Jules put it down.

"That's dumb, Jules," I said. "What a waste of ten cents! At least we could keep it as a souvenir for the club."

"Let's leave it," he repeated. I could tell he really felt like leaving it, so I didn't argue. When Jules made up his mind, there was no sense trying to change him.

Very early the next morning as I was getting ready for school, the doorbell rang.

"Answer the door, please," my mother called. It couldn't be Jules or Sam, I thought. They always hollered for me and I hollered for them in our special way: both hands cupped to the mouth, very loud, like a song —"Yo, El-leee!" Jules and Sam would never ring the bell. And it was too early for visitors or salesmen.

When I opened the door I had to blink my eyes to make sure I was awake. No one was there. Then I looked all around, and suddenly I noticed a small white envelope sticking out of the mailbox. I opened it. Inside there was no note, no name—just a dime. Who could have left a dime?

I stepped out onto the porch and looked around the Square. It was a wonderful sunny morning. Birds were hopping around the mall. It was so early that no one was stirring yet—no one, that is, except Mrs. Lukesh, all by herself, going into her house and closing the door behind her.

Four

"I *knew* Mrs. Lukesh would appreciate the airplane!" Jules whispered to me for the third time later that morning when we sat at our desks in school. "I just had a feeling she would."

"You were right, Jules," I told him. "And that's ten cents more for the club." I folded up the envelope with the dime in it and put it in my desk as Miss Fenster began handing out our brown music books.

"We have just enough time to run through our song before we go down to the auditorium to rehearse with Miss Swan," said Miss Fenster. Miss Swan was the special person who came to teach music once a week. She had twinkling eyes and a graceful way of moving her hands. Singing lessons were fun, even though we did have to do some pretty strange things.

"Let's warm up with a few sequentials," Miss Fenster said. Sequentials were exercises that were supposed to warm up your voice. I never understood why we couldn't just get right down to business.

"As you know," Miss Fenster went on, "we are to appear first on the program on June 8, when the awards are presented. Miss Swan wants us to sing 'Watchman, What of the Night?' " Everybody was happy because "Watchman, What of the Night?" was our favorite song in the whole brown music book.

"What does it mean?" Sam wanted to know. " 'What of the night?' "

"It's a poetic way of asking the watchman what the weather is," Miss Fenster said. She usually tried to answer Sam's questions patiently. Maybe she felt sorry for him the way I did.

"Open your books to page 52," Miss Fenster said, "but first let's hear the second sequential." She blew on her pitch pipe. "Do-mi-sol, re-fa-la, mi-sol-ti, do!" Miss Fenster's voice sounded like a crow's compared to Miss Swan's, but the kids who still didn't know their sequentials followed her. There were seven sequentials altogether, and when you could sing them all, solo and by heart, you got a gold star on the Sequential Chart.

"All ready now, page 52!" Miss Fenster blew the opening note on the pitch pipe.

> Watchman, what of the night?
> The stars are out in the sky,
> The merry round moon will be rising soon,
> For us to go sailing by . . .

"That sounds a little weak today," Miss Fenster said when we had finished. "I hope you'll sing out for Miss Swan in the auditorium." I figured it didn't matter whether we did or not. Miss Fenster's voice always drowned everybody out anyway.

"Line up, two by two," she told us. "Miss Swan is expecting us now." I lined up with Jules as my partner. But just as we got the sign to go out the door, a siren wailed outside, and the school bell sounded three long and three short rings.

"Oh, my heart!" said Miss Fenster. "This is an air raid drill," she went on calmly, as if she had just received word directly from President Truman. "There is to be absolutely *no talking*. March single file to the basement opposite the gymnasium door. Crouch, facing the wall. Good citizens *do not talk* during air raid drills!" Miss Fenster led us to the basement with its special odor of dampness and peeled paint. In every direction came long lines from the other classes, with no sound but the dull shuffle of hundreds of feet.

"Bzzzzzz, here they come," Sam said, as soon as Miss Fenster rounded a corner. Sam was always doing imitations of dive bombers. I gave him a disgusted look.

"Whooosh . . . vrooom . . . duck! Here comes a Kamikaze! Suicide attack by the Japanese!"

"Shush!" I whispered. I wasn't just being a goody-goody. Kids from other lines were looking at Sam. He was going too far for an air raid drill. I pinched my lips together as a signal to him to be quiet. We passed the boiler room and rounded the corner.

"Rat-tat-tat-tat-tat!" Sam pretended to man the anti-aircraft. "Rat-tat-tat-tat-tat!"

"Sam!" I warned. Mrs. Rice, the principal, was leading the line coming toward us.

Sam turned around and looked at me. "Rat-tat-tat,"

he said deliberately, just to mock me.

"Shut up!" I yelled at him. Somehow the words came out much louder than I expected. In the silence of the gray basement, with students now stopping on both sides of the corridor, my cry rang out. Clapping my hand over my mouth, I knew it was too late. Mrs. Rice, directly opposite me, frowned and stared. I quickly fell into crouch position, but when I looked up over my shoulder, standing behind me was Miss Fenster. She could only look at me and shake her head hopelessly. I turned my face to the wall. Well, that finishes the Citizenship Award for me, I thought.

After the air raid drill and all during the singing rehearsal in the auditorium I was feeling pretty awful. I thought of telling Miss Fenster that I had just meant to keep Sam quiet, but that would have made me a tattletale. I couldn't stand kids who were always telling the teacher, "It was so-and-so's fault!"

Walking by myself on the way back from the rehearsal, I noticed that Sibby was trailing behind me.

"Wait up," she said. I waited. We walked together until we came to the girls' lavatory. Sibby motioned for me to go in, and she followed me, an ugly look on her face.

"How come you didn't nominate me yesterday?" Her hands were on her hips.

"I couldn't nominate back," I said. She was a puny thing, and silly too, but she made me nervous just the way her mother did.

"You could of got Jules to do it."

"I asked him. Jules wouldn't."

"Jules would do whatever you ask. Jules *loves* you."

"He *does not!*" I protested. "I did ask him, and he wouldn't. That proves it."

"If you kissed him he would." Her eyes glimmered. "I know what I'll do," she smirked. "Too bad you lied to my mother, because now I'll have to get back at you."

"What do you mean?" I pictured her telling Miss Fenster about our walking on the rafters.

"I'm going to tell Jules that you love him and you want to kiss him."

"Don't," I said weakly. All this talk about kissing was bothering me more than the idea of Sibby telling lies about me to teachers. Kids were always joking about boys liking girls and vice versa, and most of the time we knew it was joking, but I could see that Sibby might know how to make Jules believe her. He would be embarrassed. Some day I wanted to grow up. I wouldn't even mind looking like some famous movie star—Betty Grable, maybe. I wouldn't mind kissing then. But now I just wanted to be Jules' friend. Sibby could spoil it. She knew she had found my weak spot.

"I'm telling Jules that when you come to my house, you always talk about him. I'm saying that we sit in the barn and whisper about what boys we like, and you say you like him. I'm telling Jules you wish he would kiss you."

"Sibby, if you do, I'll . . ." What could I do to her? Beat her up? That would make me look silly. I couldn't threaten her about boys and kissing—she liked that kind of teasing. Then suddenly I remembered an old saying that my father always recited: "You catch more flies with sugar than with vinegar."

"Sibby," I changed my tone. "If you promise not to, I'll let you in our club."

She took her hands off her hips and looked at me with interest. "What club?"

"It's called the Milford Square Good Citizens' Model Airplane Club, but you can join even if you don't live on Milford Square."

She narrowed her eyes. "Who's in it?"

"Jules, and Sam, and a boy named Tim Feeney who goes to St. Agatha's and some little kids on our street."

"All boys?"

"Well, just about." I hadn't thought of it that way before.

"Okay, I'll join," she answered quickly.

"And you promise not to tell Jules what you said?"

"I promise. When's the next meeting?"

"I'll let you know." She sure was anxious.

"You could have meetings and not tell me. How will I know?" That kid didn't trust anybody.

"It's called the Good Citizens' Club, isn't it? The whole purpose is to do good, not to trick people." Even though I said it quite nastily, it seemed to satisfy her.

"Well, okay. Will the others let me join?" That might be a problem, I was thinking, but I would work it out.

"Yes," I told her. "They like you." I don't know why I said that—it was a lie. Sometimes I just felt like telling lies to make things easier. Anyway, Sibby smiled almost

as much as the day when Miss Fenster had said that
Mrs. Lane was a generous mother.

"Might you be having a meeting today?" Sibby asked.

"Wait for me after school," I told her, "I'll find out."

"Ellis," she hugged my arm, "you're my best friend."

Lucky me, I thought.

Jules and Sam weren't too happy when I told them
about inviting Sibby into the club, but I threatened to
quit if they didn't let her join. I was still burning mad
at Sam for getting me into trouble during the air raid
drill. Besides, I convinced them more members meant
more money, and the whole point of the club was to
get money for the war effort.

"Wait for us in the playground," I told them when
school was out. "Sibby's calling her mother to tell her
about the club meeting."

"Hurry," Jules said. "We're going straight to Windsor Avenue."

"What for?"

"For magic tricks. The club's going to give a show to
make money. We're going to see Mingus."

The Mingus Magic Shop was one of our favorite
places on Windsor Avenue. Going straight from school,
the long way around, took us past Priscilla's Candy
Store, the library, and the Rialto Theater. Naturally on
the telephone Sibby's mother had said she could go to
the club meeting. If somebody had invited Sibby to play
after school in California Mrs. Lane would probably
have been glad to pick her up.

When we passed by the school yard of St. Agatha's, we saw Tim Feeney.

"Want to come to see Mingus?" Jules called.

"Wait a minute." I could see that his school friends were trying to convince him to stay with them. Tim always played with the Catholic school kids separately or with us separately. It was like he lived a double life.

"Okay, wait up," he yelled. One of his school friends thumbed his nose at Tim as he ran to join us.

"What do ya do at that school?" Sam asked, as Tim fell in step next to him. "Do you pray, or what?"

"Well, yeah, sometimes," Tim said. "It's a regular school." He seemed embarrassed. I thought it was rude of Sam to ask questions like that.

"*Our* school is *regular* school," Sam said, making it worse.

Jules looked at Tim. "Isn't it that you believe God is everywhere, so you shouldn't ignore him anywhere, not even in school?"

"Yeah," Tim said. He looked surprised that the explanation was so simple. "What're you going to Mingus for?"

"We're buying tricks for a magic show for the club," I told him. "When school's over, we're going to have a show and charge money. This is Sibby," I pointed to her.

She was smiling as usual, runny nose and all. "Hi," she said.

Tim nodded and looked at Jules. "A girl in the club?" he asked.

"You dope," I sighed, "*I'm* a girl, and I'm treasurer."

"Oh, yeah," Tim said, "but that's different."

We made one stop before Mingus'. At the Wee Nut Shoppe mosey pans were on sale, two for a nickel. Mosey pans were caramel, like the coating of a candy apple, poured into little fluted molds. They were bad for your teeth but delicious.

"That's fifteen cents of club money going for us and not the war," I worried.

"They send soldiers chocolate, don't they?" Jules said. "That's why it's scarce here. Chocolate helps them feel better and fight better." I admired Jules for the way he always explained things so well.

The smell from Van Horn's bakery was tempting, but we didn't stop. We also went right by Weitzel's Five-and-Ten, the one place our parents had told us not to go into. Someone had supposedly once seen Mr. Weitzel, who was an old man, trying to grab a little girl, so our mothers made us promise not to go there.

"He's a Nazi," Sam said as we went by. I felt sort of sorry for Mr. Weitzel. I could see how a person who didn't like him for some reason could just make up stories to get him in trouble.

Mingus' shop was at the opposite end of the block from the Rialto and the Wee Nut Shoppe. It was in a funny, out-of-the-way building below ground level. We walked down a few steps and through a door that said MINGUS—MAGICIAN. The front of the tiny shop was filled up almost completely by a big combination counter and showcase. Inside it the tricks were displayed.

There were red lacquered boxes with hidden compartments, wands with gold tips, multicolored scarves, strange decks of cards and papier-mâché rabbits. It seemed as if nobody but us ever came into Mingus'.

We had to wait and tap on the case and clear our throats a lot before Mingus finally heard us and came from the back of the shop. Mingus didn't need a costume to look like a magician. He was tall and skinny, with black hair slicked straight back, and he had a small moustache like toothbrush bristles.

"Well, well, well, what can I do for you?" he asked, laying his palms on the counter.

"We want a few tricks to put on a show," Jules said. Mingus knew us pretty well and he was especially nice to Jules. I guess he could tell that Jules was really talented at magic.

"How much do you have to spend today?"

"We have $2.30 altogether," I said. Besides our model airplane money we had collected dues.

"We're putting on a show to make money for the war effort," Jules explained.

Mingus nodded. "I have a trick here that's a new acquisition. I'll demonstrate for you, if you like."

That's what we were waiting for. The five of us sat on a wooden bench against the wall, while Mingus disappeared into the back room. When he came out he wore a top hat and black cape that he swirled around.

"Ladies and gentlemen," he said, "to see is to believe. What you see before you is a plain ordinary can of peanut brittle. A can, that is, that *once* contained peanut brittle but is now perfectly empty—devoid of all matter." I loved the way Mingus talked. He took off the lid and showed us the bottom of the can.

"Now then," he replaced the cover and waved his wand over the can, "did I say *perfectly* empty?" His eyes flashed. "Alas," he said, "nobody's perfect." Lifting the lid he pulled out a piece of real peanut brittle. "Who would like a tasty morsel of this delectable confection?" He tossed a lump of peanut brittle to Jules, who broke off a corner for each of us.

"Now that we have disposed of that tasty tidbit . . ." he showed us the inside of the can again, "perhaps I can convince you that we now have a void container. I will cover said container with this lid." Mingus waved his wand again.

"Make more peanut brittle!" Sam shouted.

"What's that you say?" Mingus bowed to Sam and handed the can over the counter to him. "More peanut brittle? Help yourself, my good man." Sam ripped off the lid and bounced back in surprise. Out of the can at full force burst an accordion-like snake—a kind of jack-in-the-box.

"Help!" Sam cried. "I said *peanut brittle!*" Tim tossed the snake back to Mingus, who dropped it to the ground and recovered the empty can.

"Owing to scarcities resulting from the war," Mingus apologized, "it pains me to say that we have a shortage of peanut brittle. Can I offer you a substitute—something to keep up your flagging spirits?" He waved the wand and beckoned to Sibby, who lifted the lid gingerly.

Nothing popped out. All we could see was a corner of red and white silk.

"Pull," ordered Mingus. Sibby pulled the corner of material—and pulled and pulled—until she had pulled out an enormous American flag.

"Is that trick for sale?" I asked.

Mingus smiled. "Tin can complete with peanut brittle, snake, flag and full instructions is for sale."

"How much?"

"Ordinarily I charge five dollars," he said. "However, in these particular circumstances, knowing that the proceeds from a show will be turned over to a worthy cause, I am happy to offer a reduced rate. A rate, shall we say, of two dollars and twenty-five cents?"

I could tell that Jules wanted it even though it would make us broke.

"Let's take it," I said. We all watched while Mingus explained the written instructions to Jules. Then, still wearing his hat and cape, Mingus wrapped up the trick and took our money.

"It's been a pleasure to do business with you," he said. "May I present you with my card." He handed me a calling card that read:

Mingus—Magician
Performer and purveyor of
MAGIC
1309 Windsor Ave. Wissining, Pa.
Available for entertainments,
private parties, etc.
Call Chas. Wertz   WI3-1731

"I'm appearing at the Windsor Fair on July fourth," Mingus said. "Perhaps you'd like to catch my performance."

Jules and Sam said they would but that they would probably be appearing themselves in the Wissining Fourth of July parade. I didn't say anything. I was still trying to get over the disappointment that Mingus' real name was Chas. Wertz.

On the way home, while we were talking about plans for the magic show, we saw McKinley and bought a twin Popsicle from him with our last nickel. McKinley was a very old man—one hundred years old supposedly —who sold ice cream from a homemade wooden cart. It was easy to spot the cart, a big orange box mounted on wheels. Early in the morning, whenever the weather was good, McKinley pushed the cart for five miles across the Windsor Avenue Bridge to Wissining. Kids at all the playgrounds along the way knew what time to expect him. In the evening you could see him, a wrinkled little man with no teeth, pushing his orange cart back toward the bridge. Some people said that his real name wasn't McKinley at all, but that he had taken that name because he was born in the same year as President William McKinley. I looked it up once and found that that would have made him 102 years old.

We shared the Popsicle five ways as we stopped to wait for the train to pass at the corner by the Rialto Theater. Sam and Tim waved to the man on the caboose, and Jules, Sibby and I looked at the Rialto's

Coming Attractions. The next movie was going to be *The Purple Heart,* about an American soldier who had his tongue cut out by the enemy because he wouldn't talk. I wanted to remember to tell Miss Fenster to be sure and see it.

At the top of the hill that led from Windsor Avenue down to Milford Square we all held our breath as we always did. On the corner stood the Gruen Funeral Home. A funny feeling came over me as we passed Gruen's and crossed to the opposite side of the street. Maybe it was thinking about McKinley being 102 years old, or maybe it was seeing the poster for *The Purple Heart,* or maybe it was just the spooky look of Gruen's with the sun going down, but suddenly I got scared. I felt nervous, as if some bad news was about to come. I even looked at Jules' face to see if there were any signs that he had received a message, but Jules, holding on to the new magic trick, looked calm and happy. I let out my breath slowly as we rounded the corner and moved over a little closer to Jules as we walked down the hill.

Just before we got to the McConagy's house I let the others get ahead of us and I took Sibby aside to tell her about Les' being missing in action. I wanted her to understand why we tried to be quiet in the McConagy's house and why Mrs. McConagy might look sad. I might have known, though, that Sibby would get all interested in the details so that I had to shush her at the door.

"Shut up!" I whispered. "Mrs. McConagy might hear you!"

"But what did the telegram *say?*" she kept on.

"I think they say something like, 'The War Department regrets to inform you . . .'—something like that. Now shush!"

Jules, Sam and Tim had already gone inside and down to the basement. Mrs. McConagy stood at the door smiling and wiping her hands on her apron as we came up on the porch.

"Hello, children," she said.

"She doesn't look sad," Sibby whispered to me so that I had to punch her in the arm to be quiet.

"This is Sibby Lane," I said loudly, to make sure I would drown out any other dumb remarks.

"Won't you girls have something to drink before you go down to the basement?" she asked us. "How about some iced tea?" They consumed more iced tea in Jules' house than in a restaurant. Jules' father was always yelling out the door before supper to ask if he wanted iced tea. Even though Jules always said yes, his father kept on asking every night, even if Jules was at the far end of the square.

I would have liked some iced tea, but I was shy about saying yes. I thought it would be more polite to say no first. "No, thanks," I said.

"Well, then," Mrs. McConagy untied her apron and took it off, "run down to the cellar. The boys are already down there."

Sibby jostled my elbow as we went down the cellar steps. "Why did you say no to the iced tea?"

"I thought she'd insist," I said miserably. I had to admit I was thirsty and disappointed.

"You're dumb," she sighed with disgust.

No sooner had we gotten down to the cellar, where Jules was unwrapping the magic trick, than I heard the sound of an automobile horn outside.

"That must be for me," Sibby said. "Come up with me, Ellis."

That simp couldn't even walk to the door by herself. I followed her up the steps and out onto the porch. A car had stopped by my house. It must be her father's handyman, I thought.

"Come on, Ellis," Sibby pulled me by the arm. "When's the next meeting?" Sibby skipped over to the car and opened the door. I stood behind her, peering through the side window.

"Hello, Ellis," said a voice. I felt weak and limp. It was Mrs. Lane. I stayed where I was, unable to move any closer to the car.

"Hello," I said softly. Sibby hopped in, and Mrs. Lane leaned across her to look at me. I stared at Mrs. Lane. What would she say? What would she do to me for not nominating Sibby?

"It was so nice of you," she smiled, "*so* nice of you to invite Sibby to join your club." I tried to stammer something polite, but I couldn't say anything that made sense. I couldn't believe it. Mrs. Lane was acting as if nothing had happened—as if we had never had the discussion about nominating Sibby for the Citizenship

Award. Her face was an explosion of smiles. I had thought that the world would end for her if I didn't nominate Sibby, but it seemed as if to Mrs. Lane the whole thing has been just another conversation. I still felt weak in the knees looking at her—some courageous person *I* was. But in a way I felt sorry for both of them. No wonder Sibby was such a simp.

When the Lane's car had turned out of Milford Square, I went back down to the McConagy's cellar to join Jules, Sam and Tim. They had finished practicing the new trick and had pulled out the *Omega,* Les' high school yearbook and an album of Les' photographs. The four of us sat on the floor looking at them. Les looked so handsome in his graduation picture—the same picture I had in my notebook—that it made me feel sad again.

"Let's see the baseball team." Sam turned the pages. Les had starred at first base for Wissining High.

"Think Les'll try for the major leagues when he comes back?" Tim asked.

"Maybe," Jules said. "He likes the St. Louis Cardinals."

I edged in closer. "Let me see the other one," I said. Farther on in the book there was another shot of Les sitting under a tree with a beautiful girl named Judy. I had seen the picture a lot of times, but I never got tired of looking at it. I wondered whether Judy wrote letters to Les and how she felt now that he was missing in action. Across the bottom of the picture she had written in big round handwriting with circles dotting the i's,

"Dear Les, 'Don't sit under the apple tree with anyone else but me . . .' Always remember our song. All my love, Judy." Sam snorted as he read the inscription and went on to the photograph album, but Jules and I looked for a long time at the picture of Les and Judy.

Five

The final weeks of school passed quickly, as we worked on our World War II scrapbook, took the big *Weekly Reader* test and rehearsed with Miss Swan for the end-of-the-year program.

"June 8—remember," I told my parents. Everybody was coming. I purposely didn't mention that I was up for the Citizenship Award, because I didn't want to sound conceited, and I was sure I wouldn't win anyway, thanks to stupid Sam. I tried not to think about the award at all. I told myself it didn't matter. Still, as much as I tried to put it out of my mind, the award was one of the things that haunted me as I lay in bed at night.

There was another thing that haunted me sometimes too. On certain nights that same feeling that I had had on the way home from Mingus' would come over me while I was waiting to fall asleep—a feeling that something was going to happen, and I had no control over it. When the feeling came I would try to bury my head in the pillow and imagine pleasant things, but soon I would look up in spite of myself and see shadows on the wall, the hulking clothes tree in the corner, and worst of all, the bookcase. The bookcase was a big piece of furniture with glass doors on each shelf. It had belonged to my Grandma Carpenter, who had died when I was a baby. The long shelves, the dark wood and the glass doors made me think of a picture I had seen of Snow White in a glass coffin. In the dark I imagined that someone was inside the bookcase. Then I would start to think about my Grandma Carpenter and my two grandfathers I had never seen, the Gruen Funeral Home up the street and what it must be like to be dead.

Since I was old enough to remember, nobody I knew had ever died. Sam's real mother had died, but I had never known her. Sometime, I figured, death would have to come close to me. Maybe even now Les Mc-Conagy was dead. And some day my Grossie would die —she was already pretty old. I couldn't imagine what it would be like if Grossie didn't come to visit us anymore or tell us stories about when she was little. That reminded me that Grossie hadn't come to bring us things from the farmers' market for more than two weeks. Maybe something was wrong. Suddenly everything seemed dark and scary and uncertain. I tried to get my mind off people dying by thinking of McKinley who was still selling ice cream even though he was 102.

On nights when the bad feeling didn't come over me I would start thinking instead about the Citizenship Award. While I was trying to fall asleep I would predict who would win. Sometimes I was sure it would be Sally. All the teachers liked her, and a lot of boys would vote for her. Maybe people would think she must be a good

citizen because her father was a major in the Army.
Then again, I figured that boys *and* girls would vote for
Bruce. He had the highest rank in collecting tin cans.
We got badges to sew on our sleeves for bringing in the
most flattened tin cans to be melted down for the war.
Bruce was a General—he had brought in 2,354 cans.
And Bruce would be sure to vote for himself—that
would boost his support. John might win if everybody
thought the way I did. He never got in trouble and he
wasn't stuck up.

When I thought about my winning I got confused.
Sometimes I lay in bed picturing the auditorium filled
with people, and Mrs. Rice announcing my name as
winner, and my mother crying because she was so
happy. I had never actually seen my mother cry because
she was happy, but that's the way it always was in books.
Other times I pictured Mrs. Rice announcing my name
and my walking up on the stage with my head lowered.
Then just as she handed the plaque to me I would say,
"Thank you very much, Mrs. Rice. I'm sorry—but I
can't accept the award. I don't feel that I truly exem-
plify those qualities that you all admire." The audience
would be shocked, but they would understand, and they
would applaud even louder than if I accepted it, because I was so modest.

The whole Citizenship Award was getting on my
nerves. I wished it would be over. Probably *nobody* had
voted for me—not even Sibby.

On the evening of the end-of-the-year program the

auditorium was jam-packed by eight o'clock. My mother had wanted me to wear a fancy dress with things on the shoulders that looked like fish fins, but I insisted on wearing a plain pale blue dress that everybody said matched my eyes. Everybody who was singing "Watchman, What of the Night?" was supposed to sit up front, so I sat down in the only empty seat in the first row, and my parents and Mickey went to find seats in the back. The whole town was there: parents, teachers, older brothers and sisters, Pat the policeman and somebody important from the Army. A special ceremony was going to be held in honor of Jack Laubach, a Wissining boy who had been killed in the war. His parents were going to present a flag to the school in honor of Jack. Mr. and Mrs. Laubach were sitting with the Army officer right across the aisle from me. They must have felt sad, while all around them were people laughing and talking as if nothing bad could ever happen.

Just after eight Mrs. Rice, the principal, stood up on the stage and raised her hand for silence. Mrs. Rice was a widow whose two children were students at the school. The Rices were just two regular kids. It was hard for me to picture kids going home and having the principal as their mother.

"Welcome, honored members of the military," she began, "Mr. and Mrs. Laubach, parents, teachers, and last but not least, students. We have come together tonight to crown the school year with this grand finale and to do honor to worthy students, those who are with us, and"—she glanced at the Laubachs—"and those who are not." I thought it was rude of her to remind them about Jack.

"Our program tonight will begin with 'Watchman, What of the Night?'" sung by the older students accompanied by Marybeth Gruen and directed by Miss Amanda Swan." Everyone clapped a lot for Miss Swan, who was very popular. "I don't know if Miss Swan wants me to tell you her little secret or not," said Mrs. Rice, leaning toward the audience as if she were going to whisper it. Miss Swan looked surprised.

"In a way the news is disappointing, because it means that Miss Swan will not be with us next year." The kids in the audience groaned. "But the children of Walla Walla, Washington will be very happy," Mrs. Rice went on brightly. "Miss Swan will be teaching music next year in Walla Walla, where she will be moving with her husband-to-be, Mr. Warren Fritz." Even though I joined in the applause I was upset. First of all, Wissining would probably get a much worse music teacher, and second, I felt sorry for her that she had to change a beautiful name like Swan to Fritz. I was in a pretty nervous condition anyway, just from thinking about the Citizenship Award.

"Watchman, What of the Night?" sounded wonderful, and when Miss Swan blew the pitch pipe at the end, we were on the exact note we were supposed to be. Next, a girl from fourth grade played "Nola" on the piano, and then Mr. and Mrs. Laubach and the officer came up on the stage. There were tears in Mrs. Laubach's eyes when Lieutenant Frazier, the officer, made a speech about how brave Jack had been. After she presented the new flag to the school we all saluted and observed a moment of silence for Jack. The whole ceremony made me think about Les. Maybe someday the McConagys would be giving a present to the school in honor of Les. I had never known Jack Laubach personally, but I felt like crying anyway.

My stomach started feeling strange as soon as the awards part of the program began. My whole insides felt as if they had melted and as if heat rays were going out to my arms and legs and making them numb. I strained to try to see my parents, but the auditorium was too crowded.

"The first award," said Mrs. Rice, "goes to a girl who is well known and liked. In this case the prize is for her penmanship. Miss Mienig will present the Good Writer's Medal." There was some clapping. Meany—that was our nickname for Miss Mienig, who taught art and hand-writing—had taught in Wissining so long that the audience gave her a hand just for still being alive.

"It gives me great pleasure," Meany said, "to present this year's Good Writer's Medal to a young lady who writes in a clear, legible hand. She has truly mastered the fine points of the Palmer Method. A member of the Good Writers' Club for some weeks now, she is Miss Sally Cabeen." The audience cheered. I wondered if the evening would start and end with Sally. The Citizenship Award, I knew, would be last.

There were lots of other awards—for growing the best victory garden, drawing the best fire prevention poster, writing the best composition on "Why We Are in the War," and things like that. Bruce won an award for his 2,354 tin cans. Jules got a blue ribbon in a model airplane contest. And then came the Good Citizenship Award.

My teeth were chattering. I saw Mr. and Mrs. McConagy, but I still couldn't catch a glimpse of my parents. From the row behind, Sibby leaned over and pinched me. "Good luck," she said.

"The winner is . . ." Sam was horsing around, "the winner *is*—Sam Goff!" he whispered.

Mrs. Rice closed her eyes and waited for complete silence. "This is the high point of our evening. The older students have selected from among their number the one whom they think is the best citizen." Please don't talk long, I thought. She mentioned all the good points the winner was supposed to have—leadership, patriotism, and courage. Sally Cabeen, at the end of the row, was calm and smiling.

"And so, without further ado," said Mrs. Rice, "I present to you the winner of the 1944–45 Citizenship Award—Ellis Carpenter!" Even though I had pictured various scenes in my mind while lying in bed, my reactions were slow now that the moment had finally come. I sat motionless in my seat.

"Ellis!" Sibby shouted as the clapping started. Everyone in the row was staring at me. Sibby poked me furiously in the back. "Ellis, get up there!"

Dazed, I stumbled up the steps of the stage as the applause grew louder. Had I dreamed of making a speech to turn down the award? Impossible—I couldn't have gotten out one word. Mrs. Rice held out the plaque in one hand and put her other arm around my shoulders. While she read the inscription aloud she patted me warmly. Had Mrs. Rice forgiven me for making noise during the air raid drill? Or had she been outvoted by the other teachers and was just being a good sport about it? Probably she was still mad at me and didn't think the award meant anything now that I had won.

My head was spinning with all the selfish, cowardly, and unpatriotic things I'd ever done—the incident in the barn, being afraid of Mrs. Lane and Mrs. Rice, spending war stamp money for Popsicles and candy, yelling "shut up" during an air raid drill—and I felt as if a very heavy weight were on me. Whether or not I *was* all those things, now I'd have to try to be them. The winner, Miss Fenster had said, was supposed to be a model. Could you be a model and still be a regular person that people liked? As I walked off the stage, and parents and friends began to congratulate me and hug me, I was glad I had won, but I wasn't completely happy.

In the pit below the stage the school orchestra started up its concluding number, "Don't Sit Under the Apple Tree," one of the most popular songs of the war—the song title, in fact, that was written under the picture of Judy and Les in the yearbook. As I scanned the auditorium for the faces of my mother and father the words kept going through my head. *Don't sit under. Don't sit. Don't.* I guessed there would be a lot of don'ts for a person who was trying to live up to the Citizenship Award.

I hurried toward the back of the audience to find my parents and Mick. Seeing me coming, my father smiled.

"Wonderful!" he said as he hugged me.

"Where's Mother?" The expression on his face changed. "Where's Mom?" I repeated.

He drew me aside, away from the people who were pushing their way out. "She left early. Grossie is sick."

"Sick? Sick with what? Who called her? Who knew Mom was here?" I couldn't understand what illness was so bad that my mother would have to run off suddenly.

"Don't worry, don't worry." My father held my shoulders. "Grossie's in the hospital, but she'll be coming home. Mother knew today that she would have to leave early, but she didn't want to spoil your evening. She was awfully sorry to miss the awards. She knows you won. Miss Fenster called her this afternoon."

"But what's the matter with Grossie?"

"She's had an operation. We'll know more about it after Mother talks to the doctor. Uncle Frank picked her up and took her to the hospital." My father took my free hand and with his other hand grabbed Mickey as he ran by. "I mean it now." He fixed his eyes on me. "Don't worry. Let's celebrate the award on the way home with an ice cream sundae." Sundaes were a special treat. We wouldn't be celebrating with a sundae unless everything was going to be all right.

"What a fine daughter you have," someone said to my father. When I turned around I saw that it was Mrs. Laubach and the lieutenant.

"That's what I think too," my father said.

"Thank you," I said, blushing. The evening had been so exciting and confusing. I hadn't seen Jules since before the award. I wondered if *he* thought I deserved it. Even though I was scared about a lot of things, there was also a lot to be happy about, I thought. School was over; the vacation was just beginning. There would be club meetings and the Fourth of July parade. And winning the award—that at least *should* be making me happy. I looked again at the inscription on the plaque in my hand. "To a student who exemplifies qualities of leadership, citizenship, and courage—Ellis Carpenter." I sure hope so, I thought.

Six

As my father, Mickey and I walked in the door, I knew right away that my mother wasn't home yet. An empty house sends out signals even before you enter it. I hung the Citizenship plaque next to the bookcase in my bedroom, in a spot where I could see it easily but other people couldn't. I figured that even though I didn't want to show it off, it wouldn't be a bad idea to have it around as a reminder to myself of what it stood for.

"Mother may be home very late," my father said. "I think you'd better get into bed."

I lay in bed thinking of everything that had happened during the day. First I pictured over again in my mind the award presentation. I hoped that I hadn't looked too silly and embarrassed on the stage. That was one thing about Sally Cabeen, she always looked and acted the same, as if she lived her whole life being ready to be called up for an award. I admired that, in a way. How would Sally feel about me now that I had won the award, I wondered. I wouldn't have minded being Sally's friend, but she acted as if she thought I was immature because I played with boys. Well, it didn't matter. Jules and even Sam were much more fun than Sally.

Even though it was late, I couldn't fall asleep. I kept expecting to hear my mother come in the door. What could be wrong with Grossie that could take my mother away so suddenly? And why didn't adults tell kids about serious things like illnesses, I wondered. *Anything* was better than not knowing. I thought of Grossie lying all covered up with a white sheet in the hospital. It was hard to picture. Usually Grossie was so strong and full of life. She was always telling me stories about the things she and her good friend Mary Ellis had done when they were girls . . . things that got them into trouble but were funny when you told about them years later, like playing hooky from school and dressing up to look old enough to get a job. I was close to Grossie, and suddenly the thought that she might be very sick brought on my scared feeling. The reflections on the glass panes of the bookcase didn't help me, either. "It's just a bookcase," I kept telling myself. But the eerie, hollow feeling inside me didn't go away. What would everybody think, I wondered, if they knew that the courageous award winner was lying in bed afraid of a bookcase? Finally, forcing myself to turn my back to it, I dropped off to sleep.

When I woke up the next morning Snow White's coffin had turned back into a piece of furniture. The sunlight streamed through the window, and there stood my mother examining the Citizenship Award.

"Congratulations," she said. "I'm sure sorry I missed it. Miss Fenster telephoned me, you know, and Daddy told me all the details about the program."

"How's Grossie?"

My mother hesitated for a minute and then sat down on the end of my bed. "She's doing all right. She's going to be in the hospital for a few weeks, and then she'll go home to her house."

"What's wrong with her?"

"She's had an operation. It was pretty serious, but the doctor says she's strong."

"But what's *wrong* with her?" I insisted.

"It's . . ." My mother hesitated again. "She's going to get better." I couldn't tell whether or not my mother was keeping anything from me. If Grossie were going to die, would Mom tell me the truth? I felt like asking more questions, but I was afraid I'd upset Mom, and I was afraid of what the answer might be.

"During these next two weeks I'll be visiting Grossie in the hospital every day," she said. "I'm sure I can count on you to take care of yourself and to watch Mick when I go into Windsor, can't I?"

I nodded. "Can I go too?"

"No, they don't allow children in the hospital. But you can see her just as soon as she comes home. She misses you."

"I was wondering why she didn't come to our house for two Fridays."

"She hasn't been feeling well. She went into the hospital two days ago, but I didn't want to worry you, especially before the awards program." Maybe Mom wasn't telling me more now because she didn't want to worry me.

"I think it's wonderful about the award," Mom looked at me seriously. "I'm very proud." Then she laughed and pulled off the sheet. "Now hop out of bed! First day of vacation!"

I had almost forgotten. Jules, Sam and I had agreed to have a club meeting. Before I had finished my breakfast, I heard Jules and Sam on the porch calling me.

"It's great that you got the award, Ellis," Jules said to me right off. He looked as if he meant it.

"Wait'll they find out." Sam paced around me like a detective cornering a criminal. "When they find out your grandmother is a Nazi, they'll come and take the award back."

"My grandmother's sick," I said. "She's in the hospital." Most kids would feel bad if they made mean jokes about a sick person, but Sam didn't care.

"I guess there's lots of places to hide Hitler inside a hospital," he said. "The doctors there could do an operation on his face to disguise him." Even though I gave Sam a dirty look, I had to admit that a trick like that might work, if Hitler were still alive.

"You're stupid," I said. "Germany's not even our enemy anymore. They gave up. They're sorry Hitler started the war."

"You two arguing won't solve anything," Jules interrupted. "I have ideas we can start working on for the club."

I turned my back on Sam. "What ideas do you have, Jules?"

"The whole club should dress up and go together in the Fourth of July parade," Jules said, "and when they hold the money scramble in the swimming pool on the Fourth we should contribute all we get to the club." I nodded.

Jules went on. He was loaded with ideas. "Tomorrow let's go to the creek and pick watercress to sell to people."

"Pfoooeee!" Sam made a face. He hated the taste of the watercress that grew in patches on the banks of Wissining Creek.

"*You* don't have to like it," I told him, "just so long as grown-ups buy it. What'll we do today, Jules?"

"How about a show right here in the neighborhood?"

"I know what," I suggested. "Let's go around when all the neighbors are home tonight and ask them if they want us to sing for a penny."

"Cri-men-ent-lees!" said Sam. That was a favorite word of his when he was disgusted. "Singing for a penny!"

"It'll be easy," I insisted. "We can just sing 'Playmate,' and 'Anchors Aweigh,' and maybe 'Watchman, What of the Night?' "

"The little kids don't even know that one."

"I'll teach it to them," I said. "We'll play school, and I'll teach them."

"Play *school*—ugh. On the first day of vacation?" Sam looked at me as if I were crazy.

"Don't worry," I told him. "We'll just sing for fun. There won't be any sequentials."

In the afternoon while we were sitting on my front steps practicing songs, Willie Pflug came waddling from his house on the next street. Willie was fat and babyish, even though he was practically our age.

"Hey," he puffed. "Hey, you kids. Somebody's moving into the house next door." When we looked, we could see through the backyards that a big van had pulled up next to Willie's house.

"Let's go!" Sam tore across the mall and through the yards to Willie's street. The rest of us followed.

"Do they have any kids?" Jules asked Willie.

"Don't know yet," Willie said. "My mother says they come from New York."

The whole club, including Tim, Ruthie and Mick, watched the movers carry things into the house.

"They've sure got *old* furniture," Sam said, as we watched the men squeeze a fancy cabinet through the front door.

"Those are antiques," Jules said. "Antiques are valuable."

"Hey, look at that!" I pointed to a rolltop desk with flowers on it. "I bet there's a girl!"

"Ugh," Sam said. He turned away in disgust.

That evening at seven o'clock the Milford Square Good Citizens' Model Airplane Club, with everybody present except Sibby Lane, met at the lamppost on the mall. We had invited Sibby, but she had a piano lesson.

"We're going to go around," Jules explained, "and ask the neighbors if they'd like to hear a song. Ellis will hold out the tin can when we finish, and we'll hope that they make a contribution to the war effort."

Following Jules, we made the rounds of the houses with Sam trailing behind. "I'm not singing," he said.

We must have picked a good time because most of the families in the square were sitting out on their porches. At the Shoppe's house they wanted to hear us sing "Playmate," a song about a little girl who couldn't play because her doll was sick. Their grown daughter kept laughing at how cute Ruthie was, and she got her to sing a solo, acting out the words.

The Shoppes appreciated it so much that they gave us a nickel. Ruthie was smiling, and I personally think it was the first time that anybody ever paid attention to her in her life.

"Dumb song," Sam said under his breath as we walked to the next house.

At the Goff's house Sam disappeared completely, but Ruthie sang "Bell-bottom trousers, coat of navy blue," about a little girl who admires a sailor, and when she grows up she falls in love with him. At Tim Feeney's house, his old grandmother who lived with the Feeneys, wanted us to sing "Ave Maria," but we didn't know that, so we sang "Mairzy Doats" instead. Mairzy Doats was a nonsense song, but it made sense if you sang it very slowly.

Grandma Feeney probably didn't understand, but she clapped anyway, and the Feeneys gave us another nickel.

After we had gone to all the other houses I thought Jules might suggest singing for Mrs. Lukesh, but when I pointed to her door, Jules shook his head no.

"Her lights are out," he said. "We might bother her." As far as I could remember, Mrs. Lukesh *never* had lights on. She must have spent every evening alone in her dark, creepy house. I hoped when I got old, I'd turn out to be full of life like Grossie and McKinley, and not a crab like Meany, our writing teacher, or a person who loved only grass, like Mrs. Lukesh.

Lightning bugs suddenly appeared, the street lamp in the middle of the mall went on, and I heard my father calling from the porch, "Time to come in!"

I grabbed Mick by the wrist and started pulling him toward home.

"Don't forget tomorrow," Jules said. "Let's leave early for the creek."

"Let's not take the little kids," Sam called. He tried to get rid of his half sister Ruthie whenever he could.

"I'm going," Mick said.

I felt like saying "No, you're not," but I was pretty sure my mother would expect me to take care of him while she was at the hospital, so I just gave him a mean look. Mick could be a pain. I dragged him the last few feet onto the porch where my father was waiting.

"Okay, you two, up the wooden mountain!" my father said. That's the way he always put it when it was time to go to bed.

Seven

The following day was perfect for the mile-long walk to the creek. Sibby met us at my house. Willie was never allowed to go anywhere out of his mother's sight, and Ruthie stayed home because Sam's stepmother had a day off from her defense plant.

"You'll take Mickey with you, won't you?" my mother asked. I felt as if I didn't have any choice.

"Do I have to?"

"You don't have to, but I wish you would. It won't be much longer that I'll ask this of you." I always wished my mother would just say, "You *have* to." That made things easier than leaving it up to me. Whenever she left a decision up to me I felt terrible if I didn't do the thing she wanted.

"C'mon, dumbbell," I grabbed him by his skinny wrist.

"Now, Ellis," my mother gave me a look, "I'm sure Mickey won't stand in the way of your having fun. Be careful," she said, as I picked up our lunch bags and walked out the door.

Wissining Creek, which curved through the town and

emptied into the Schuyler River, was one of my favorite places. In most spots the creek ran shallow enough to wade in up to the knees. There wasn't any place along the creek that was very deep, which was why we were allowed to go there by ourselves. On one side of the rippling water lay sunny fields of tall grass and daisies. On the other side were woods full of evergreens and pine cones, umbrella plants and jack-in-the-pulpits, rocks and moss.

"Let's head for the springhouse," Jules said, as the six of us—Tim had come too—walked along the path that ran parallel to the creek. The springhouse, a low building made entirely of stone, wasn't in use. Maybe, years before, someone had lived nearby, but now the springhouse was just a decoration in the grassy field. No one could go inside; there was a heavy rusted chain across the door. But the low, rounded shape and the rough stone surface made it perfect for climbing over.

"I'm for eating lunch on top of the springhouse," Sam said. "Right now." Even though it was still early, we all scrambled up on the roof and took out our sandwiches. Mick had been dragging behind us the whole way, just as I had expected. I had to push him up onto the roof from the bottom, while Sibby pulled him from the top.

"You're a pain," I told him, as he let pieces of egg salad fall out of his sandwich onto the rooftop.

"Let's go wading as soon as we eat," Sibby suggested. She wasn't anxious to start working.

"Save the lunch bags," Jules said. "We have to have

something to carry the watercress in. I brought a jar, but it won't all fit in there." Since we had left home Jules had been carefully juggling a Mason jar, the kind our mothers used to preserve homemade things from victory gardens. We finished our lunch.

"Last one down to the creek is a Nazi!" Sam yelled, as he leaped off the roof. Mickey balked at jumping, and we only got him to come down by Sibby's pushing and my catching him in my arms. The two of them took off, leaving me trudging behind. The others, minus their shoes and socks, were already wading in the creek.

"You're last! You're the Nazi!" Mick stood on the bank and giggled at me.

I was annoyed. "Get lost," I said. "You give me a bigger pain than a Nazi." I ignored him and stepped into the creek.

At first the cold water tingled and made our ankles numb, but soon we were all in up to our knees.

The stones in the creek bed were slippery, and it was a trick to keep balance.

"Watch it," I warned Mick. "Two bits you'll fall in and get your pants wet."

Everybody had forgotten about watercress for the time being. Sibby had spotted a cluster of cattails, and Jules was trying to scoop minnows into his Mason jar.

"Hold it, Jules," I shouted. "Let me get you something." I climbed out of the water to the spot where I had put down my lunch bag. Leftover sandwich crusts made perfect minnow bait.

"Good," Jules said, as he held the bread close to the mouth of the jar. "Hey, I got one." The minnow looked lonesome and confused inside.

"Yo, Jul-lee!" Sam yelled just at that moment from downstream. "Yo, El-lee!"

"What do ya want?"

"Come here and see what I see." Sibby, Tim and Mick followed us as we slid over stones to where Sam was perched on a flat rock. "Up there." Sam pointed into the woods. "There's that pipe Bruce Brown was talking about." Some yards up the bank, buried in the hillside—its opening partly camouflaged by roots and branches—was a cement sewer pipe big enough to walk into. Bruce had once bragged to our class that he had walked from one end of it to the other.

"Let's go up and look at it," Jules said. He left his jar on the flat rock, and even though I was annoyed at Mick, I helped him across the sharp stones between us and the bank.

The soft earth crumbled as we picked our way up the incline. There was a bit of a rocky shelf at the opening to the pipe. A thin trickle of water ran over the shelf and down into the creek. The six of us stepped inside. It was like a tunnel with no end. The first few feet were light enough for us to make out the damp cement over our heads, the rusty trickle of water under our feet, and the features of each others' faces. Beyond that was sheer blackness.

"Yoooooooo!" shouted Sam suddenly. We all jumped. The echo of Sam's cry rang through the pipe. "There's a pit inside, you know," he said in a hushed voice.

Usually I didn't believe half the things Sam said, but this time I had heard the same story from Bruce Brown. There was supposed to be a great round hole in the floor somewhere in the pipe.

"If you fall in it," Sam's voice sounded hollow, "there's no hope. It's filled with garbage and rats."

"Who says?" I had never heard of that.

"Everybody knows it. That's why it's called a *sewer* pipe."

"Is that true, Jules?" Sibby asked him. "Are there rats?"

"I don't know. Let's walk in a little and see what the pipe is like."

"Jules, I don't want to." I didn't want Jules to think I was scared, but the thought of dropping into a pit of rats was horrible.

"Then don't," he said. "I'm only going to walk with a stick in front of me, so I can tell if there's a pit or not." Jules stepped out of the pipe and picked up the first good-sized stick he could find. It was an inch thick and taller than he was.

"I'm going in," Sam said. He liked to act big. "I'm telling Bruce we found the pit and walked around it."

"I'm going in," Sibby said. She was getting pretty courageous since she had started hanging around with our club.

"I'm *gone!*" Tim stepped in front of all of us and walked forward until we could see only a dim outline.

"Help!" he cried in a fake voice, as if he were disappearing into the pit.

"I'm going," said Mick.

"Well, stay behind me," I told him. "You're too little for this stuff." If everybody else was going into the pipe I had to go too. Otherwise they would think I was a coward.

"Let me go first, Tim." Jules advanced, tapping the ground ahead of him with a stick like a blind man. Tim and Sam inched along behind him. I tried to hang back, but I couldn't let Mick go without me.

"I told you to stay behind me!" I yelled.

"Off we go, into the wild, blue yonder . . ." sang Sam. Usually he hated to sing.

"Ugh, the walls are slimy!" Sibby must have figured that you couldn't get into much trouble walking on the curved part of the pipe. Just like in Sibby's barn, the danger lay in the middle. Tim was making hooting noises up ahead. All the voices bounced off the walls and made the pipe sound like a madhouse.

"Shush, everybody!" Jules shouted all of a sudden. The pipe grew deadly quiet. Over our shoulders we could see the circle of light at the entrance, but we could barely see each other. The only sound was the slight scraping of Jules' stick against the cement. Jules held still, and all was quiet. Then we heard a faint rustling and a drip, drip.

"Help!" screamed Sam, "we're at the pit!" Nobody waited to decide if he was right or not. We all turned

and ran back as fast as we could until we breathed
the fresh air outside the pipe.

"You scaredy-cats!" Tim said as we caught our breath.
"That wasn't anything!" Still, the sunshine felt good.
Jules stepped off the rock ledge and put a twig between
his teeth.

"Remember why we came to the creek?" he asked.

"For watercress!" I said. Before anybody could suggest going back into the pipe I jumped off the ledge,
and clinging to roots and rocks, I led the way to the
water below.

"I see some!" Jules cried, and we followed him to a
spot where the water ran cold and clear under shade
trees. The watercress grew right there in the creek.

I ate my first handful, washing it off in the creek
water. It made my tongue burn slightly, in a pleasant
way.

"Leave it wet," Jules called, "it stays fresher that
way."

We had gathered quite a bit of watercress before I
looked around and first noticed that Mick wasn't there.
Before I said anything I turned in a complete circle,
checking every spot in view.

"Anybody seen Mick?" I tried to ask calmly, but my
voice cracked.

"Mick?" Everybody stopped picking and looked up.

Jules paused and thought. "I don't remember seeing
him at all since we started gathering watercress."

"Did somebody help him down the hill after we came
out of the pipe?" I asked.

"Not me," said Tim. The others shook their heads. Jules calmly waded over to the bank nearest the woods and laid down his watercress.

"You don't think he could still be up there, do you?" I asked him.

"We'd better check," he said. The rest of us came out of the creek.

"The first thing to do," Jules said, "is to call him very loud. No sense chasing in the wrong direction." He cupped his hands in front of his mouth. "Yo, Mick-kee!"

"Yo, Mick-kee!" we shouted in unison. The only answer was the hum of insects in the grass and the cry of one lone mourning dove. I faced the other way and called again.

"Let's check different places," Jules suggested. "Ellis, come with me up to the pipe. Sam, go to the springhouse. Tim and Sibby, walk across the fields to the road. Keep calling his name a lot and meet back here in ten minutes."

It was lucky that Jules took charge because I was in a panic. My imagination started running wild, and I felt weak and sick.

"He wouldn't have gone back into the pipe by himself, do you think, Jules?" I asked him as we climbed the hill. I had trouble keeping up, because suddenly I couldn't breathe right.

"I doubt it. Maybe he's playing around the shelf."

"But then he'd hear us yelling."

"Well, maybe the wind is blowing the other way." I knew Jules was just saying that. There was no wind blowing at all. Making our way up to the pipe seemed like hurrying in a dream. The faster I tried to go, the longer it seemed to take. Every minute or so we heard the cry of "Yo, Mick-kee" but no answer.

"Has Mickey ever gone off before?" Jules gave me a hand up to the next stump.

"Not that I know of. Once he and Ruthie ran away, but they only went to the end of the square, and then they came back for cookies."

"He wouldn't hide for a joke, would he?" We pulled ourselves up on the rock shelf.

"He'd better not!" I said, "I'd kill him!" And then, realizing what I had said, I started to cry. "Call him, Jules, I can't."

Jules stood inside the opening. "Yo, Mick-kee!" All we heard was a faint sound like the last water draining from a bathtub. Jules called again.

"Don't," I sobbed. "It's worse to *not* hear him answer!"

"He couldn't fall in the pit." Jules came over to where I was crouching on the shelf and sat close to me. "There *isn't* any pit," he said softly.

I looked in his eyes. "You said there was. So did Sam and Bruce Brown. There *is so* a pit." But I hoped he was right.

"There are plenty of places around here for a kid to hide or get lost." Jules got up.

"Get lost," I repeated. "I told Mickey to get lost! When I was mad at him before for being so slow and being such a pain. Could he have thought I meant it?"

"Little kids can be dumb," Jules said, shaking his head, "but I don't think so. Everybody knows what 'Get lost' means. Besides, even if he did go off because of what you said, we'll find him. You can't hide out forever in these woods. It's not like some jungle in the Pacific. Let's call again—one, two, three, Yo, Mickkee . . ."

I turned around and looked below, where I caught a glimpse of Sibby and Tim, by now near the road. Only a corner of the springhouse could be seen through the trees, and I couldn't see Sam at all. Every second that went by made me feel more helpless, frightened and sick to my stomach.

"Maybe there's an empty well or something that he could have fallen into," I said. "Or a trap. Or maybe he got bitten by a snake."

"He'd yell if that happened," Jules said. "Maybe he went *up* the hill here, instead of down. I wonder what's at the top." Above the pipe the incline was sharper. There was no path at all, but by hanging on to saplings and rocks it was possible to climb. "Let's go," Jules grabbed my hand.

"Aren't ten minutes up?" I asked. "You said to meet in ten minutes."

"We'll just check this one place before we go down."

"Mick couldn't climb up here," I said as we made our way up the sheer cliff.

"Jules," I jerked his hand to make him look at me. "Have you gotten any message about Mick?"

"Message?"

"You know, message about whether he's safe."

"Oh, that." He bit his lip and looked away for a second. "Not exactly a message, but a feeling. Let's go up on top."

"Is he safe, Jules?" I gripped his hand hard.

"I'm pretty sure he's safe." He let go of me to reach for a higher rock.

I wasn't sure how I felt about Jules' messages. Even though I trusted him more than anybody, the messages seemed like magic, and I didn't really believe in magic. I didn't object to magic tricks like the ones Mingus sold—they could be explained. But knowing things before they happened was scary, and I didn't like to think it was possible.

On the rest of the way up the cliff I started picturing different terrible scenes: finding Mick badly hurt; suddenly coming upon his body, propped against a tree, maybe; facing my mother and telling her that Mick disappeared because I had said, "Get lost." How would my mother feel if Mick wasn't found? Didn't she have enough worries already, and hadn't she warned me, "Be careful"?

Jules reached the top before I did. "Hey!" He shouted with such surprise that I thought he had found Mick. "It's the street! The top of the cliff is just a regular street!" He pulled me up the last few feet. I didn't know the name of the road, but I recognized it as a spot behind John Elting's house. It was strange that we hadn't thought about the fact that the creek and the woods were, after all, right in Wissining. Even though

Mick wasn't there, it seemed a little less frightening to realize that the pipe and the springhouse weren't so far from civilization.

"Mick-kee!" I shouted. And then, far away, where the street turned down toward the creek and the fields, I saw Sam waving his hands and running in our direction.

"Did you find him? Did you find him?" I called, as I headed to meet Sam. When we were close enough to see each other's faces, we slowed to a walk. I thought I might faint from being out of breath.

"Did you find him?" I panted.

Sam smiled. "Yup. Pat's got him." He threw himself on the grass by the road. "Whew!" he sighed. Pat was one of the town policemen. He was known for being nice to kids.

"Where did *Pat* find him?"

Sam's chest heaved from his running. "Mick must've walked sideways through the woods instead of down to the creek the way we went. Then he got scared 'cause he didn't know where he was. Pat found him on the road near the springhouse. He's sitting in Pat's patrol car."

"That dope," I said. But I laughed and kept on running until I got there. Mick was sitting calmly in the front seat of the car playing tic-tac-toe with Pat.

"Here's the criminal, Ellis," said Pat, who knew the name of everyone in town. "You weren't worried about him, were you?" I laughed and cried at the same time.

"Mick, you jerk!" I stuck my head in the window,

"what did you get us worried for like that? I'm telling mother!"

"Go ahead," he said, drawing an X between two O's. That kid could be a pain.

Pat drove us all home in his patrol car. I guess he could tell we had been pretty upset. The only one who wasn't upset was Mick.

"Why did you go off like that?" I asked him, half relieved and half angry.

"Nobody waited for me," he said. He wasn't at all sorry. He was happy in fact, sitting up front with Pat and fooling around with the two-way radio. I knew I'd have to tell my mother about the incident, especially since she would probably see us arriving in a police car. When we drove up in front of our house, everybody piled out, and we thanked Pat a lot for helping us. As Pat pulled away Jules clapped his hand to his forehead.

"Remember what we went for?"

"Watercress!" We all groaned. By now it must have been all wilted on the bank of the creek. The minnow was probably still there too, stranded in the Mason jar.

"We could go again tomorrow . . ." Tim said hopefully.

"*Count me out!*" I said, grabbing Mick by the wrist and pulling him into the house.

Eight

Before we knew it the early days of vacation had passed —days spent swimming, and practicing magic tricks and checking every day to see if the new family had moved in yet next to Willie's house. Suddenly it was the Fourth of July. The Fourth of July was a very important holiday in Wissining, almost as important as Christmas. Since gasoline was rationed, it was hard to go away on vacations, and everybody in the whole town came to the parade, the contests and the big dance on Fourth of July night.

About eight o'clock in the morning the club gathered in front of my house to get dressed in our parade costumes. We had decided that the whole club would go dressed as marines landing on the Pacific island of Iwo Jima. I thought I looked pretty good. I was wearing a pair of Jules' old khaki pants and a work shirt of my father's that was the same color. I had sewn the patches I won from collecting tin cans onto my shirt sleeve, so it looked like a real uniform. Jules had also lent me a pair of hiking boots that once belonged to Les. When

I tucked my hair under Mick's toy Marine helmet, it was pretty hard to tell I was a girl.

It wasn't easy borrowing the Marine helmet from Mick, who wanted to wear it himself. That kid had done pretty much whatever he liked since the day he had gotten lost at the creek. He had told my mother that we left him, and she had blamed me for going near the sewer pipe. The only way I got the helmet from Mick at all was by sitting on him and tickling him.

Jules and Sam carried the McConagys' flagpole between them, and Tim held the sign we made that read: FROM THE HALLS OF IWO JIMA TO THE SHORES OF WISSIN-ING. Sibby wasn't going to be in the parade because her parents were taking her somewhere on a picnic, and Willie's mother wouldn't let him march in the hot sun.

"Good luck!" My mother said, as the six of us started off. "I'll see you tonight." She was going to be away all day. There was good news: Grossie was coming home from the hospital.

By the time we arrived at the playground where the parade was starting people were already lined up on both sides of the street. Some kids were wearing very fancy costumes. Freddy Barth, the grandson of the richest family in town, wore a beautiful George Washington suit with lace cuffs and a silver wig. Sally Cabeen, I had to admit, looked like a movie star in a dress made out of net material. She was supposed to be the Spirit of Liberty. A lot of bicycles and tricycles had red, white and blue crepe paper woven through the spokes of the wheels and flags attached to the handlebars.

"Hey, Ellis!" called a voice. I saw somebody dressed as an American Indian and I had to look twice to be sure that it was Bruce Brown. "Guess who's going to win the next Citizenship Award!" He pointed to himself and pretended to pat himself on the back. This was the first time I had seen him since the awards program.

The high school band played "Over hill, over dale, we will hit the dusty trail, as those caissons go rolling along!" As we marched through Wissining the whole parade stopped and the band played a patriotic song whenever we passed by a house that had a blue star or a gold star in the window. A blue star meant that they had a son still fighting in the war; a gold star meant that a son had been killed in action. I thought a lot about Les, especially since I was wearing his old boots.

The part of the Fourth of July that I liked best took place after lunch—the money scramble. Someone in Wissining, who kept his name a secret, contributed lots of coins to be thrown into the town swimming pool. It must have been the Barths who gave the money. No one else was that rich. You could keep all the coins you dived for, and Jules, Sam, Tim and I had agreed earlier to hand our money over to the club.

The swimming pool shimmered in the afternoon sun. The bottom was clean and blue, with wide black lines that looked magnified through the water. Wait until I get those coins, I thought.

"All contestants will now line up at the side of the pool for the annual Fourth of July coin dive," said a voice over the loudspeaker. I searched for Jules and Sam, but I couldn't see them anywhere. In fact, I hadn't seen much of them since the parade. Two high school boys, both looking like Tarzan of the Apes, shoved in on either side of me at the edge of the pool. While I tried different stances for getting off a good dive the lifeguards walked behind us, hurling coins—mostly pennies—over our heads into the water. The sky rained money, as if we were in a fairy tale.

"Contestants ready." My chest hurt from taking in so much air. "Take your mark." I covered my ears to dull the sound of the blank shot.

"Go!" The starting gun cracked. The two Tarzans jostled me with their elbows as they sprang out over the water. Flashes of spray glistened, bubbles rose from beneath the surface, blurred forms shot along the black lines under the water. I stood rooted to the matting by the edge of the pool. What am I waiting for! I thought.

Taking in an enormous gulp of air, I jumped in feet first. Stupid me, I thought. Dive down! Even though the water was only neck deep, I had trouble getting to the bottom. Just as I turned myself downward my lungs felt as if they were going to burst, and I had to surface. Finally I touched bottom and saw something round, but it turned out to be a pebble. Bodies bumped and shoved me under the water. Once when I had the tips of my fingers on a penny someone bigger snatched it out from under me.

At last I saw a clear space and something that looked like a coin. Filling my lungs, I did a surface dive. It *was* a coin, and it was *silver.* I shoved hard against somebody coming from the right and gulped for air. Nosediving, I got my hand on it. A quarter? A dime at least? Oh, no! A penny! One of those 1943 silver-colored pennies that they made because copper was scarce. Not even made of real silver but of some ugly mixture with aluminum in it. As I sucked in air for the next dive, the sound of a whistle rang in my ears. The scramble was over. I had found *one penny.*

"That's too bad," my father said as we sat at the supper table. "But you remember, don't you, what Grossie wrote in your autograph book?" I did remember. It said, "A good name is rather to be chosen than great riches." Well, I guess I was pretty lucky. Ellis was a good name. But when it came to the Fourth of July money scramble, I had hoped for great riches.

Jules, Sam and I walked together to the playground in the evening. I had long since taken off my marine outfit and was wearing my favorite pair of shorts for the dance. Jules was especially quiet. I wondered if something had happened during the day—if maybe he had gotten a message.

"Where's your penny from the scramble?" Sam sneered at me. "Are you splitting it three ways?"

"I'm giving it to the club like we agreed," I said glumly.

"What do you mean," he screwed up his face, "*we agreed?* Who said anything about giving the money to the club?" Sam had ended up with forty-five cents in the scramble.

"We all did. Don't you remember?"

"Nuts, I never agreed."

"Sam, you liar." I felt like punching him.

"Only goody-goodies like *you* agreed. Goody-goodies who win citizenship awards!" He twisted his words so that the award sounded like something terrible.

"Jules, didn't we agree to hand over the money?" Jules had found twelve cents in the pool. "Jules?"

He seemed to be thinking about something else. "I . . . I don't remember," he said. I couldn't believe it. Jules never forgot things and he almost always backed me up.

"I mean the *swimming money,* Jules." I poked him.

"I don't remember." There was a tone to his voice that made me drop the subject.

"You going to play hide-and-seek during the dance, Jules?" I asked. We younger kids usually hung around at dances just to watch and get free refreshments, or to play outside.

"I don't know," he said as if he were annoyed. He looked strange. Maybe he had eaten too many hot dogs and Popsicles.

The dance was held at the playground under a long pavilion with a cement floor. For the Fourth of July all the picnic tables were pushed aside and phonograph music floated through the night air. Most of the high school kids had come with dates. As I looked at them laughing and talking, I wondered what it would be like to wear cute short dresses, hold hands with a boy and comb my hair a lot like the older girls at the dance. For us younger kids the dance was mostly a chance to fool around and drink pink lemonade.

Everyone was there. Bruce Brown was showing off as usual. Suddenly Bruce looked toward the entrance to the pavilion. "Hubba, hubba!" he said. That meant a beautiful girl must be coming. I turned around, and so did Jules and Sam. Sally Cabeen, wearing a white dress, her hair down her back in soft curls, had just walked into the pavilion with Philip Helmuth.

"Hubba, hubba, woo-woo!" Bruce called and wiggled his eyebrows up and down until he caught Sally's attention.

"Hi, Bruce," she smiled. "Hi, Jules."

"Hi, Sam," Sam shouted.

"Oh, Sammy, I didn't see you! Hi! And there's Ellis . . ."

For somebody with everything else in such good shape, she sure had poor eyesight. I was sort of sorry I had worn my shorts. Everybody looked so dressed up.

"Ellis, I meant to tell you," she leaned her head forward, close to Philip, supposedly to see me better, "I'm so glad you won the Citizenship Award."

"I'll bet she is," Sam mumbled under his breath, which was exactly what I was thinking.

"Thanks," I said. Sally and Philip drifted off, and I turned to Jules. "Want to go outside and start hide-and-seek?" I asked him.

"Not now," he said, fading back to sit on a bench at the edge of the pavilion. The dancing had begun. I hoisted myself up on a table near where Jules was. It was fun to watch the older kids jitterbugging to the fast numbers and dancing very close when they played something romantic like "I'll be seeing you in all the old familiar places." At the far end of the pavilion I thought I saw Judy, the girl who was in the yearbook picture with Les. Maybe it wouldn't be so bad to grow up and have boy friends who'd write you letters, and wear your hair long and shiny, and dance close.

Then I saw something that almost knocked me over. Right in the middle of all the high school couples stood Philip Helmuth and Sally Cabeen, swaying with their arms wrapped around each other. We had all been forced to take ballroom dancing lessons in the school gym—lessons that usually ended up in a riot that we called "boys chase girls." But now Philip and Sally were holding each other and looking into each others' eyes in a way that we hadn't learned in school.

I turned to Jules. "Look at that," I scoffed. He nodded solemnly. Sam came and sat down quietly next to him. The two of them stared at the dancers.

"Want lemonade?" I asked. They both shook their heads no. As I walked alone over to the refreshment table I saw Bruce Brown tapping Philip on the shoulder to cut in on the dancing. Philip argued for a second and then let Bruce go off with Sally. I hadn't been very surprised at seeing Philip and Sally on the dance floor— Philip loved girls, and Sally was always going around acting like a pinup girl. But Bruce? Was he going to start loving girls too?

Sipping my lemonade, I walked slowly back to where I had been sitting. The floor was crowded with teen-agers, soldiers in uniform and parents. Philip Helmuth must feel bad, I thought, having Bruce cut in on him like that. And then I saw that I was wrong. Philip wasn't feeling bad at all. Instead he looked as if he was having a great time. He and Marybeth Gruen were swaying back and forth with their eyes closed, while the voice on the record sang:

> I only know that love is grand,
> and the thing that's known as romance is
> wonderful, wonderful in every way, so they say.

Marybeth Gruen, ugh! I thought. I wouldn't want to dance so close to the daughter of an *undertaker.*

When the music stopped there was a lot of clapping, laughing and talking. Bruce, Philip and John Elting came over to Jules and Sam, and I could see the whole bunch of them whispering.

"Go ahead," Sam snickered, "ask her. I dare ya." I couldn't tell what they were talking about. Meanwhile Sally and Marybeth were leaning against a post talking to some older boys. Sally threw back her head and laughed a lot. The two of them, Sally and Marybeth, in their cool summer dresses, with their blond hair flowing, looked like an advertisement for Pepsi-Cola.

As the music started up, there was a rush of activity around Sally and Marybeth. It seemed as if every boy in Wissining had just discovered them. One of the Tarzans who had pushed me at the pool swept Sally

away. John Elting, who had never pushed anybody before in his life, danced off with Marybeth. Philip, Bruce,
Jules and half a dozen others stood with their mouths
open, watching in disappointment. Jules! Sam had
dared Jules to dance with Sally!

Suddenly I felt sick. The Fourth of July had started
out as such a good day. We had looked so good in the
parade. The money scramble had been fun, even if I
hadn't gotten a lot of coins. I had been so happy just a
little while earlier because of wearing my favorite shorts.
But now everything was different. Shorts! Nobody was
wearing shorts except me. Everybody else was wearing
fairy-tale dresses. Maybe boys didn't mind me in their
clubs, but when it was time to act like grown-ups, boys
looked at Sally, not me. Maybe it would be that way
from now on. Boys weren't interested in girls who won
citizenship awards.

Even though Tarzan had taken Sally away, the others
didn't give up. One by one a steady flow of boys cut in
on Sally. Finally Jules got his turn. It could have been
my imagination, but it seemed as if she smiled more
and snuggled closer to Jules than to all the rest. I was
getting sicker. Maybe it was all the hot dogs, Popsicles
and lemonade.

I glanced around to see if anyone was looking at me.
I would even dance, I thought, if somebody asked me.
But nobody did. Every time another couple went out
on the floor and every time Sam or Jules laughed or
made a remark I shrank farther back in my corner. The
record ended.

"I danced with her!" Sam ran up to Jules and pounded him on the back. "Hey, Julie, you owe me a nickel!" I couldn't believe it. Jules was betting good money so that Sam would dance with Sally.

"Not *yet,* I don't," Jules said. "Remember the other bet." I tried to catch his eye, but Jules walked away toward the refreshment stand where Sally was drinking lemonade. The next thing I knew, I saw Jules and Sally leaving the pavilion together. Outside the sky was black, and the woods beyond the pavilion looked spooky.

"Where are they going?" I motioned to Sam. My curiosity was killing me.

"Outside," he grinned. "I promised Jules my whole forty-five cents if he kissed Sally."

I felt as if the cement floor had dropped away. "Is he going to?"

"Sure!" Sam said. "Jules *loves* Sally." I didn't wait any longer. As soon as Sam looked the other way I hurried out of the pavilion. Just as I set foot on the gravel path at the bottom of the steps I saw again a face I had seen earlier. Even though it was quite dark I could pick out a soldier in uniform with his arm around a girl. While I stood there he stooped and kissed her for a long time like in the movies. I knew now for sure that the girl was Judy, who had once written to Les, "Don't sit under the apple tree with anyone else but me."

Things could change awfully fast in this world, I thought. I turned away from Judy and the soldier and ran in the dark as fast as I could, but I didn't actually cry until I was home in bed.

Nine

The next morning when I woke up it was raining hard. I lay on my back, staring at a big stain on the ceiling and feeling pretty bad. The door opened and my mother came in to see if I was awake.

"I'm sick," I said. She came over and put her hand on my forehead, but I guess it didn't feel very hot.

"Eating too much junk," she muttered. A person could be lying in an ambulance, covered with blood, with broken bones sticking out all over, and my mother would be shaking her head and saying, "Comes from eating too much junk."

"Okay, stay in bed," she said on her way out of the room. Probably she thought I would argue and leap right up, but I fooled her.

"I think I will stay in bed." I nestled down in the sheets and pretended to go back to sleep. She stuck her head back in the door.

"Do you really feel bad?"

"Yes," I said. That was the honest truth.

"I'm sorry." She paused. "Then you'll have to wait until tomorrow to go visit Grossie."

"Oh, she's home!" I felt ashamed that I had forgotten. I had been thinking so much about myself. Maybe I should insist even now that I was well enough to visit Grossie today.

"Yes, she's home," my mother said. "How about going to see her tomorrow. Why don't you rest today?"

That settled it. I leaned back and started thinking about things. First I noticed that the spot on the ceiling was shaped like a man with a beard, and I wondered whether it was true that God knew everything and decided who was good and who was bad. If there was a heaven was it hard to earn, like the Citizenship Award, or could anybody who was around get in, like our Model Airplane Club? If God was as kind as He was supposed to be He probably welcomed everybody in, but on the other hand somebody perfect like God might have pretty high standards.

Then I started thinking about the Fourth of July and about winning and losing. That's all anybody cared about. Bruce, Sally, John and I had cared about winning the Citizenship Award. I had wanted to beat everybody out in the money scramble. Sally was probably trying to win all the boys and make them love her. Even the whole country of America was trying to beat Japan now, the way we had beaten Germany and Italy —because they had been trying to beat us first.

Most games were fun, but lately I was seeing how games could hurt people. I had gotten hurt in Sally's game. But that was nothing, I realized, compared to Les' getting hurt or even killed in the war. I knew that

the war was different from other games. We had to win
the war because the Axis Powers—the enemy—had been
too greedy and were killing innocent people. But I
wished the whole thing could be over and that everybody in the whole world, including myself, could stop
caring so much about winning.

Thinking about all that serious stuff made me feel
like getting my mind on something else, so I lay
around the whole morning reading a Nancy Drew mystery book. It wouldn't be bad, I thought, to grow up to
be a girl detective. Of course Nancy Drew had a head
start because of her father being Carson Drew, well-
known criminal lawyer, but maybe an ordinary person
could also get into that kind of work.

After lunch I tuned in soap operas on the radio. Even
though a lot of sad things were happening on all the
different programs, I still got interested. Somebody, for
instance, was on trial for murder, but he couldn't remember if he'd done it, because he had amnesia. In
another serial Mary Noble, "Backstage Wife," had a
husband who was a matinee idol. Mary kept worrying
that he would fall in love with a beautiful young actress.
Whenever one of the stories got to an exciting place
the announcer would interrupt to try to get you to
send a dollar and a box top for a beautiful simulated
pearl brooch or some other piece of junk. The last soap
opera I listened to was called "When A Girl Marries,"
about a girl named Joan. If getting married brought
you all the trouble Joan had I couldn't see why any-

body would do it. I ended up wondering if Jules would marry Sally. It was a pretty depressing day.

"Here's fifty cents," my mother said the next morning. I was to go by myself on a bus and trolley car to Grossie's house in Windsor. "Ten cents for the bus each way, five for the trolley, and twenty for mad money. Put it in a safe place."

My mother always gave me "mad money," which was supposed to be for an emergency, but which I usually spent on things to eat. I put the change in a coin purse and tucked it in the back pocket of my shorts. I was glad to be going somewhere on my own. I felt a lot better than the day before, but I wasn't in the mood to see anybody from Milford Square or anybody at all who was my age.

"Grossie will be resting," my mother said. "There's a practical nurse there today to take care of anything she needs. You help too. Try not to let her get up."

"Does she look the same?"

My mother hesitated for a second. "Yes, but she's been very sick. She's thinner. Tell her what you've been doing. Tell her about the award." My mother walked me to the front porch. "Be careful now, Little Red Riding Hood. Don't talk to any big bad wolves, and don't forget to telephone me when you get there."

I walked up the hill to the Gruen Funeral Home to wait for the Windsor bus. When it came I paid the driver ten cents and took a seat in the front next to a window. Luckily nobody I knew was on the bus because I didn't feel like talking. It was fun to ride by all the familiar places on Windsor Avenue and look at them in a whole different way—as if I were a stranger seeing them for the first time.

At the corner by the Rialto Theater we stopped for a train. Sometimes when the train stopped there kids would try to cross over the couplings between the train cars. For a second I thought I saw Sam Goff standing on a coupling, but the train moved on before I could tell for sure if it was Sam. When we passed the magic shop I looked for Mingus, but I didn't see anyone. Probably he was still appearing at the Windsor Fair. The only person I did recognize on the whole trip across the bridge was McKinley, who looked almost like a dwarf as he pushed his orange ice-cream cart through the middle of the truck and bus traffic.

Once we had crossed the river the scene was different. Windsor was a city. Shops and office buildings were crammed next to each other for blocks and blocks: the Army-Navy store, drugstores with high stools at their counters, the stamp and coin shop. On the corner by Windsor's largest department store stood a vendor selling hot pretzels. My mouth started watering for a pretzel so badly that I got off the bus at the next corner and walked back to buy one. Willie Pflug's mother wouldn't let him eat soft pretzels because she said the seller's hands were dirty, but I didn't care. I munched slowly on my pretzel and took in all the sights and sounds as I walked toward the trolley stop by the farmers' market.

I hadn't meant to go inside the market, but when I looked through the doorway the bustle and excitement and the delicious odors pulled me in. Since it was Friday all the farmers had come from the country with their vegetables, fresh-killed chickens and home-cured Lebanon bologna. Most of the farmers and their chubby, rosy-cheeked wives spoke Pennsylvania Dutch. Every now and then I caught a word I understood, but mostly I just listened to the singsong of their chatter. I stood for a second in front of a bakery booth.

"Want a *fastnacht,* little girl?" a big woman in an apron asked me. Her voice rose up and ended back down again in the Pennsylvania Dutch way when she asked a question. The homemade doughnuts, called *fastnachts,* looked delicious.

"I'm not sure I have enough money," I said.

"There nah, take one." She handed me a fat, sugar-powdered *fastnacht* wrapped in a napkin and waited until I took a bite. "Iss good, ain't?" I nodded. "No money," she said, shaking her head and waving her finger back and forth at me. "For free it iss today. You tell Mother that Schwenner's *fastnachts* iss best, yah?" I smacked my lips to make sure she knew how much I appreciated the treat. Schwenner's *were* best.

I wiped the powdered sugar off my hands as I walked to the corner to wait for the trolley car. It was more interesting to stand on the street in Windsor than back in Wissining where you knew everybody. At the stop a woman and her little boy were already waiting for the car.

"Does the car stop here for Berk Street?" I asked her.

"Yes," she said. "Where are you going?"

"Out there. Berk Street. To my grandmother's."

"You don't live round here?"

"No, I live in Wissining."

"Oh, that's where the rich folks live!" I nodded. I supposed she meant the Barths. They sure were famous.

Her little boy was hanging on her arm as if it were a swing. "Now you mind!" she shouted, shaking him off.

"Money grows on trees in your backyard?" she winked at me.

"No! Not mine! Only the Barths are rich." She gave me a funny look as if she'd never heard of them after all.

Just then the trolley car rounded the corner and I reached in my back pocket for my coin purse. Suddenly my heart started pounding—the pocket was flat. I reached in the side pocket. Empty. A terrible wave of panic came over me.

"Here comes the car," the little boy said.

"Oh, my gosh . . ." my face must have shown something was wrong.

"What's that?"

"I can't find my coin purse. It was in my back pocket!" I kept feeling my shorts as if some new pocket would appear.

"You mean, you got no money?"

"No! It's lost! I had it! It was right *here*." I patted the pocket. Maybe she didn't even believe me. I felt like crying. I turned around in circles looking at the ground. The trolley screeched to a halt. Its doors swung open while the motor settled into an impatient chug-chug-chug.

"What'll I do?" I said, talking to myself. I pictured myself getting lost trying to walk to Grossie's or walking all day to get home to Wissining.

"You take this now," The woman pushed something into my hand. It was a quarter.

"Oh . . ." I hated to take money from somebody I didn't know, but just then she took her little boy's hand and stepped up into the streetcar.

"You coming?" The conductor called.

"Yes," I whispered, as I stepped on behind them. The conductor took the quarter and gave me twenty cents change. I followed the woman to her seat and held out the twenty cents.

"No, you keep it, honey. You got to get home." She pulled the little boy onto her lap and motioned for me to sit down next to her.

"But my Grossie'll give me money—my grandmother," I insisted, still holding out the change. "Once I get there she'll give it to me."

"Just for safety," she said.

After that I stopped trying to argue. Settling back on the wicker seat that made crisscross marks on your skin, I looked out the window. The trolley went along past rows of attached houses of brownstone and of brick painted red. In front of some of them women were sweeping the sidewalks.

"I must have dropped my coin purse by the pretzel man, or in the market," I said.

"That's a shame. But don't you mind." She patted my hand. I wished that I still had the pretzel or the *fastnacht* to give to her son, but I had finished them both. It was really nice, chugging along next to the woman and her son, passing by playgrounds and unfamiliar corner stores.

"I could send you the quarter back," I said hopefully.

"Don't you mind," she repeated, shaking her head. She stood up then to pull on the cord, and when we reached the next stop, I got up to let them out.

"Thanks a lot," I said. She smiled. When the trolley screeched away again I waved to her through the window.

Once I was sitting all alone on the streetcar I started feeling a little nervous about getting off at the right stop. Things like losing the coin purse made you realize that you could never be sure of anything. I thought back to all the places I had been in Windsor and tried to picture where it might be lying right then. Luckily there was only forty cents in it, but the purse itself was one I had made by hand, and I felt sorry that I would probably never see it again.

"Would you please tell me when we get to Berk Street?" I asked the conductor in a small voice.

"Coming up next," he said.

T*en*

Grossie's block was a row of brownstone houses that all looked the same. Each one had a porch that gave a clue about who lived there. Some had gliders, or hammocks or wicker furniture with thin cushions covered in flowered material. In the evenings the porches were always full of people sitting outside to enjoy a breeze and to talk to those who passed by. Now, in the late morning, there were just a few children playing on the porches as I walked towards Grossie's house. The Berger girls, next door to Grossie's, were playing paper dolls on a card table.

"Hi," I said.

"Hi, Ellis!" Dorothy, the older one, always acted as if I were her best friend, even though she saw me about three times a year. Claire, the younger one, just grunted. She must have thought her sister would quit playing with her and hang around with me.

"Want to come on up to my room and play paper dolls?" Dorothy asked.

"Sorry, I can't" I said. "My Grossie's sick."

"Why do you call her Grossie?" Claire wanted to

know. She gave me a nasty look even though she knew now that I wasn't going to take her sister away.

"It's short for *Grossmutter*—grandmother in German. My cousins started it so they wouldn't get their two grandmothers mixed up. I gotta go in now," I said.

The screen door was unlocked. First I thought maybe I should ring the bell to let the practical nurse know I was there, but I ended up just walking in. The downstairs of the house was always dark and silent, even when Grossie was well. The living room was filled with heavy carved furniture. I wondered if they were valuable antiques like those the new people next to Willie had. On the walls hung a lot of oil paintings and a number of deer heads and antlers. My grandfather had been a painter. Most of his scenes were of forests, lakes, wrecked castles and brown windmills. Together with the deer heads, they gave you the feeling of being in the middle of the story, "Hansel and Gretel." There was even one place where he had painted ivy right on the wall. Although it was dark, the room wasn't creepy but sort of peaceful.

I would have liked to sit in the living room for a while without anyone knowing I was there, but I didn't want to frighten the nurse in case she suddenly came in and saw me sitting there. Besides, I wanted to see Grossie.

"Grossie," I called, as I ran up the steps. Then I clapped my hand over my mouth. Maybe she was sleeping, I thought.

"Here!" a voice answered from the bedroom. "Ellis?"

The light in the room was dim. I drew in my breath. I had never seen Grossie sick before. Wearing a peach-colored dressing gown, she looked small propped up in her big carved bed. Grossie held out her arms to me. I ran toward her and when I grabbed her hands she squeezed mine hard.

"See how strong I am?" she laughed. Grossie spoke with a slight accent—not like German in the war movies —just a gentle sound in her throat when she said the letter r.

"You look good," I said. She did look pretty good but much thinner and paler than the last time I had seen her. Next to her on the bed lay a box of photographs, old letters and other things from the past. When she pushed aside a little blue book that she must have been reading I noticed that her hands shook. Just then the practical nurse came into the room.

"Mrs. Heard, this is my granddaughter Ellis."

"What a nice big girl!" I wasn't very big at all, but she must have been trying to be pleasant.

"Is that the child who's named for Mary?" she asked Grossie.

"Yes," my grandmother nodded. Then turning to me, "Mrs. Heard knew Mary Ellis too."

"A lovely woman," Mrs. Heard said. "So full of life. I took care of her for a time."

"Was she sick long?" I asked that partly to make conversation and partly because I had never really known what Miss Ellis had died of. I guess adults keep talk about illness and death from kids to protect them, but

I don't think that's so good. *Not* knowing things, I thought again, is almost always worse than knowing them. It was terrible, for instance, for the McConagy's to wake up each day wondering if Les was dead or alive.

"No," Mrs. Heard counted on her fingers, "Mary wasn't sick too long. About a year altogether." I thought a year sounded like forever. *One day* in bed with nothing but Nancy Drew and soap operas had been enough for me.

"I'll just leave you two alone now," Mrs. Heard said, as she picked up an empty glass from the bedside table. "Will you be wanting anything?"

"No, thank you," Grossie said. "I'm getting up in a little while. My one trip downstairs today is going to be to the kitchen with Ellis."

"Mom says you're to stay in bed," I protested.

"Let me bring you what you want," said Mrs. Heard.

"No, ma'am. I'm going to the kitchen." Grossie had a way of letting you know sometimes, as Jules did, that she wasn't about to change her mind. After Mrs. Heard had left the room the two of us settled back and just smiled at each other.

"I've been looking at the old photographs," Grossie pulled the black album toward her lap.

"I love to look at them. Let me see too." I fixed the lamp so that it spotlighted the album. The first picture showed Grossie in 1912 when she was already married with three children but still looked very young. "You were pretty," I said. Some people thought I looked like

Grossie. I hoped I'd look that good when I had children of my own.

"Do you remember these?" Grossie pointed to a series of photographs of my mother in ballet costumes. In every one Mom stood in front of different scenery that my grandfather had painted. Some of the pictures were beautiful and some struck me as being funny. In one of them she wore an Indian outfit like the one Bruce had worn in the Fourth of July parade. She was pulling back an arrow, ready to shoot at something that must have been running across my grandfather's scenery. There was a startled expression on her face that made me laugh.

"Is that how you got the deer heads downstairs?" I asked.

"You're silly!" Grossie said. "Isn't this one lovely?"

It was. Before they were married my mother and father had posed for this picture in front of a real arbor, not a painted one. There were lots of other photographs of family and friends. Some were of the whole family sitting in a semicircle in front of a painted garden with all the little children, even the boys, in embroidered white dresses. One showed all Grossie's children—my mother and my uncles—looking scrawny in itchy wool bathing suits, up to their knees in a swimming hole. There was my Uncle Frank who always gave us a quarter when he came to visit, and my Uncle Hans, who had died when he was a boy. I didn't stay on that photograph too long because I thought maybe it would make Grossie sad to look at it.

"Here's my favorite picture of Mary Ellis!" Grossie said when we turned the page. Mary Ellis stood leaning over a boardwalk railing to look at the ocean. On her head was a tight-fitting felt hat.

"She was so pretty," I said. "Didn't she ever want to get married?"

"Yes. She was engaged to marry a boy who was killed in the First World War."

"Really?" I had heard a lot of Mary Ellis stories, but I hadn't known that before. "Didn't it make her bitter?"

"Sad, yes. But she wasn't a person to feel bitterness. She had many offers of marriage from nice young men after that, but none of them turned her head." I liked Grossie's old-fashioned expressions like "none of them turned her head." I thought for a minute.

"If you lost someone in a war," I asked her, "would you stay by yourself forever?" I was thinking about Judy, Les' girl friend.

"I can't say," Grossie answered. "For Mary Ellis it seemed to be the right thing. For others perhaps not. Mary, after her loss, threw herself into her work and other interests. She was a teacher who loved her students, and they loved her. Your mother and father were her students, and they have told you that many times, I'm sure."

Remembering Judy and the soldier made me think of Fourth of July night. Suddenly, as I pictured again Jules and Sally going off into the woods, I felt a wave of something that was almost a pain. I started to say something about it to Grossie, but I decided I would never tell anyone what had happened or how bad I felt. I hoped I wouldn't see Jules soon—or ever.

"Seeing the pictures reminds me," Grossie said. "I want to give you something." She reached for the book with the blue leather cover that she had been reading when I came in.

"What is it?"

"It's a book of Mary Ellis' that she gave me and I'm giving to you."

"What's it about?"

"It's a book of poems by a woman named Emily Dickinson, who lived in the 1800s. You may like some of them now; others you may appreciate later. Mary wrote some things of her own in it too. I've enjoyed the book so much that I'd like you to have it."

"Won't you miss it?"

Grossie rubbed the cover with her thumb. "A little," she said. When I reached for the book, she took my hand again and held onto it. Her face looked tired.

"I'll lend it back whenever you want," I said.

"Good."

"Do you feel like sleeping now, or anything?"

"No, no. It's nice to talk."

"Tell me about when you were a girl. About Germany, or about when you and Mary Ellis were in high school."

"Well, let's see," she said. I guess it was hard to think of a new story. She had already told me so many. "A short time after I came to America, when we still lived in Philadelphia, Mary and I were invited to a picnic. I was shy then. I didn't speak English so well yet. Mary was already my best friend, and relatives of hers had invited us to go by horse and carriage to a picnic grove down by the river. It was a beautiful day, and all the women at the picnic had brought their own homemade pies and cakes. Each one had tried her hardest to make the most beautiful, best-tasting pastry. There were Bavarian chocolate cakes, and lemon chiffons and cherry pies, but the one I had my eye on was a cake decorated with lovely fresh strawberries. I couldn't wait to be invited to have a piece of that delicious, tempting dessert. But my mother had always told me to be polite, and aside from that, I was, as I say, quite shy." Grossie was still shy, in a way. I could picture how she must have looked at the picnic. Wearing braids, maybe, and a long dress.

"What happened?"

"Most of the other food was on the table so that every person helped himself, but when the cakes were served at the end, the women who baked them went around to each guest asking who wanted a piece. I was so worried that the strawberry cake would be gone before it was my turn! I turned down all the others, though they looked wonderful too. Meanwhile Mary had already sampled several different ones. Finally, when the woman came to me, there were just two pieces of the strawberry cake left. I remembered my mother's talk about politeness, and I didn't want to sound too eager. 'No, thank you,' I whispered to the woman.

"I was sure she would ask me again, because I was the

only one with no cake on my plate. But instead, she said 'Poor girl, no appetite!' and went right on by! I could have cried. The next two men on my left each took a piece, and that was the end of the strawberry cake! I was so shy and angry at myself that I didn't even ask for one of the other kinds, even though there were plenty left. I sat and watched Mary and the others smacking their lips and raving over the taste of this one and that, feeling miserable.''

"Poor you!" I said.

"To this day whenever I'm offered cake I say yes— but no piece has ever been as good as I had imagined the one at the picnic would be."

She sighed. "Isn't it funny. We learn something—that politeness can be carried too far, for instance—and then we go right on saying to our own children, 'Mind your manners! Wait until you're offered something before you take it! Make sure you don't take too much!' "

"The same thing happened to me the other day. Mom's always saying, 'Don't make extra trouble for somebody. Be polite!' Mrs. McConagy asked me if I wanted iced tea and I said no, even though I did!"

"Aren't we silly in our family?" Grossie said. "Some people—like Mary—aren't like that. Without being rude or greedy she could take three pieces of cake. She wasn't afraid to say yes right out to what she wanted. I admired that in her, maybe because I found it hard. I'm still a little shy."

"Me too," I said. I was thinking about the award, and how I still felt as if I didn't deserve it.

"We have to try harder to accept the good things that come to us without feeling guilty," Grossie said, as if she were reading my mind. The telephone rang.

"Oh, my gosh!" I said. "I was supposed to call Mom. I'll get it." I went out into the hall and picked up the receiver. It was my mother.

"Yes, she's in bed," I said. "We were just talking, and I forgot to call. I'm sorry." By the time I hung up, Grossie had gotten out of bed by herself. Standing up, she looked very weak.

"Mrs. Heard will help me downstairs," she said. "You run on down to the kitchen."

Grossie's kitchen, in the back of the house, reminded me of a Dutch painting I had seen in art class. Miss Mienig, our art teacher, often gave each of us our own little prints of famous paintings for "picture study." One of my favorite prints was a Dutch kitchen. Grossie's floor was of red tile, and there were blue and white willowware dishes on all the shelves. I loved to look at the little people and trees and pagodas on the dishes and make up my own stories about them. There was a huge window framing the backyard, but it was almost completely covered with vines and hanging plants, so that the kitchen, like the living room, was dark and cool. Sitting at the blue-enameled table I felt like Snow White in the dwarves' cottage—snug in the middle of a forest.

"I declare, she won't listen to a thing I tell her," Mrs. Heard said, as she followed Grossie into the kitchen. "That woman's overdoing it."

"You run off now, Mrs. Heard," Grossie was firm. "We'll just have a snack, and later I'll let you fix lunch." She sat down.

"I forgot to tell you," I said to Grossie, "that I lost my purse on the way here." Then I told her about stopping for the pretzel, about the free *fastnacht* and about the woman who gave me the quarter.

"You were lucky," Grossie smiled.

"I was careless," I said.

After lunch Mrs. Heard helped Grossie upstairs and into her bed again. I brought up some ginger ale, and as we were sipping it I remembered what I wanted to ask.

"Grossie, did you leave Germany because you didn't like Hitler?" I was hoping I could tell Sam that she had.

"No, no," she smiled. "Don't they teach you history in school? Hitler was only *born* at the time I left Germany. My father brought us here to find better work. Hitler came to power much later." I probably should have known that. Miss Fenster wouldn't have been too proud of me.

"Do you think Hitler's dead?" I asked.

"Why, yes, I think so. Of course there was some trouble being sure about his body, but I think most people agree that he's dead."

"If he escaped and came here, would you hide him?"

"Oh, no!" I could tell she thought my question was stupid. I wished that Sam were in the room so he could see what a dumb question it was. "You mean, because I was born in Germany, would I help Germany in this war? Ellis, you know I'm an American. I have many happy memories of my girlhood in Stuttgart, and I speak with a little accent, but . . . everyone sees that Hitler was a monster, including most people in Germany today. Why do you ask these questions?"

"Oh, some kids think all Germans are bad."

"But you know it's not so." I nodded. "Just as you know all Japanese aren't bad, yes?" I nodded again. "But you still feel a little ashamed that your ancestors were German, and Germany, in these years, has caused misery?"

"Yes," I admitted.

"I know how you feel. I felt so even more, when it was the First World War. I carried around a lot of shame. But there was no need for me to. We mustn't think so little of ourselves, Ellis. Now," she said, noticing my empty glass, "I see you have finished your magic drink that will turn you into a princess. Bring me my purse." She took out a dollar bill and stuck it inside my book of poems.

"It's time now. Keep your money safe, and tell Mickey hello." I hated to leave, but I could see that Grossie was tired. "Go straight home so Mother won't worry," she said.

"I'll come back soon." I sat for a second on the edge of the bed, and Grossie patted my hand.

"Good." Her voice sounded sad. "Then we'll talk some more."

"Thanks a lot for the book. I'll read it on the way home."

"Just be sure you don't pass your stop. And something I didn't say before—congratulations for your award! You're being so modest not to tell me about it."

"Oh, it's not much."

"What kind of lesson have you learned today?" Grossie pretended to be shocked. "We *accept* what we're offered and say 'Thank you very much!' "

"Okay, I forgot," I laughed. "Thank you very much."

"Go now," she said very low. As I went out the door she blew me a kiss, and I carried away with me a picture of her leaning back on the pillow and turning out the light.

In the crowded trolley car I had to stand and hang onto a strap. Every time the car screeched around a corner I was afraid the book would go flying out from under my arm. But later, when I got a seat on the bus, I flipped through the book and read some of the poems. They were pretty good. One of them talked about knowing things without proof.

> *I never saw a moor,*
> *I never saw the sea;*
> *Yet know I how the heather looks,*
> *And what a wave must be.*
>
> *I never spoke with God,*
> *Nor visited in heaven;*
> *Yet certain am I of the spot*
> *As if the chart were given.*

I guess it was like Jules feeling certain of his messages even though he couldn't explain them. I envied Emily

Dickinson and Jules for being certain of things without proof. I was usually uncertain. Some of the other poems, especially the ones about death and losing a person you love, had Miss Mary Ellis' writing around them. I was relieved to see that Mary Ellis had made out okay in life even though she didn't write by the Palmer Method.

"Did you have a nice time?" my mother asked when I got home.

"Oh, yes. Very nice. Grossie gave me a book."

"That's good," she said. Then after a second, "Jules was here."

I looked up. "Jules came here?"

"He called for you twice."

"What did he want?" I wondered if my mother knew that anything unusual was going on, but she didn't seem to.

"I don't know. He said he'd come back first thing in the morning. He said it was something very important."

Eleven

During the night I had a weird dream. I dreamed I was on the rafters in Sibby's barn and a crowd of people stood below, daring me to walk all the way across. Mrs. Lane was smiling up at me and calling, "Come now, Ellis, you don't want the children to lose their respect for you, do you?" I inched forward.

"Be careful!" Miss Fenster shouted. "Remember you're susceptible to hay fever!" I never had hay fever in my life, but in dreams people always say strange things like that. About halfway across I panicked and decided to turn back. As I turned I felt myself falling.

They say that if you dream of falling and hit bottom, you're dead. I don't know if that's true or not, but while I was falling I thought to myself, this is only a dream—I'll wake up. And suddenly there was Jules underneath the rafters to catch me. Before I could say anything to Jules I woke up. In my half-asleep, half-awake fuzziness I thought to myself, Jules must have gotten a message that I was falling.

The next morning I was reading in the newspaper about our troops getting close to Japan when Jules called "Yo" for me. I went to the door slowly and a little nervously. Since I had dreamed about him, it seemed as if Jules and I had just seen each other. Still, when I looked at him through the front window I felt as if he were a stranger. What important thing did he have to tell me, I wondered. That he loved Sally and we'd never be friends again? That he liked me better than Sally? Or that some more news had come about Les? Even though I was very curious, I didn't want him to think I was sitting around waiting for him.

"Hi," I said in a flat voice.

"Ellis," he looked at me gravely, "we have to practice the magic show. We're having it Monday." He was acting just the same as always. Was it possible that he would go back to the way things were without even mentioning the dance and kissing Sally?

"What's the important thing you had to tell me?" I asked him.

Jules looked surprised. "That's it—the show. We said we'd hold it right after the Fourth of July, didn't we? Hey, where were you yesterday?"

"Away," I said shortly. I felt like being mean. Could I be so upset about the Fourth of July dance when to Jules it didn't mean anything? I guess one thing you learned in growing up was that even your best friend didn't always know what was going on in your mind.

"Did you go to the Windsor Fair?" Jules asked.

"Yes," I lied. "I saw Mingus." I knew I shouldn't lie —I wasn't even good at it—but at that moment I wanted Jules to be jealous.

"You did? How was he?" His eyes lighted up, so that I was sorry right away that I had made up the story. It always made me sad when I saw a person being fooled.

"Mingus was good. Much better than the tricks he did for us at the shop."

"Oh, yeah? Which tricks did he do?"

"Hard ones. Ones you never saw."

"Like what? Did he say hello to you?"

"Yeah, he recognized me." I was about to make up more lies about the things Mingus had said, but I was afraid I'd get trapped later.

"Wow, you're lucky," Jules said. "Who'd you go with?" I went blank for a second.

"Uh, my Grossie . . ."

"Isn't she sick anymore?"

"My Grossie's . . . next door neighbors, this kid named Dorothy and her . . . brother." I thought it was pretty shrewd of me to get that in about a boy being with us, but Jules didn't seem to notice. "Her brother's two years older. He's nice," I said.

"Well, I wish I could have gone. I was looking for you yesterday. Sam and I decided to have the show on Monday, because they're saying the war'll be over soon, and we have to hurry, if we want our money to do any good."

I still couldn't believe it that Jules was just going on as if nothing had happened, as if there hadn't even been a dance. Had the dance been a dream too? It was all so strange. And here was Jules, talking about the magic show as if it were the most important thing in the world. I guessed there was nothing to do but to go right along with him. Maybe the whole business about kissing Sally had just been a joke. Boys were hard to figure out.

"Hey, Jules," I said feeling better about him, "you didn't hear anything more about Les, did you?"

Jules shook his head. "No, we didn't hear anything," he said, just as Sam Goff sprang over from the next porch. He must have been perched on the divider, waiting to take us by surprise. I didn't care to see him at that moment, but there was no choice.

"She's here," he said, "and is she *ugly!*" Jules and I looked at each other and then at Sam.

"Who?" we asked together.

"That *girl*. The one with the flowers painted on her desk. The girl who moved in next to the Pflugs."

"The new girl?" Suddenly I remembered the moving truck that had come on the first day of vacation. It seemed like a thousand years had gone by.

"Where did you see her?" Jules asked.

"She's sitting on her porch steps with Willie Pflug. They make a good pair. He looks like a circus fat man, and she looks like the skinny lady. She's got yellow hair that sticks out, and big glasses and she talks funny."

"She talk to you?"

" 'Greetings and salutations,' she said. That's how she talks! Honest!"

Jules made a face. "Is she a brain?"

"Probably," Sam said. "She wears big glasses. Comes from New York."

"What's her name?" I asked.

"Betsy. Betsy Harris. Hair sticks out like this!" Sam gave us a demonstration. I laughed. Usually I thought Sam was stupid for making fun of people on account of their looks, but to tell the truth, this time I was glad to hear that the new girl wasn't beautiful.

"Let's get on with the magic show," Jules said.

"Aw, come on, Jules, take a look at her. We'll get *her* to come to the show!" Sam was prancing around with excitement.

"Well, okay," Jules agreed. The two of us trailed behind Sam as he cut through the Feeney's backyard.

I had expected some kind of funny remarks from Sam about Sally and the dance, but he didn't say a word either. Maybe the two of them were ashamed of dancing with a girl, now that it was over. Well, whatever the reason, I felt relieved that I was their friend again.

"You talk to the new girl, Jules," I said. "Tell her about the show, and tell her we're charging a nickel to get in."

"Wait a minute," Sam looked as if a light bulb had gone on in his head. "I got an idea. Let's have some fun. Don't tell her right away about the magic show. First tell her we have a club, and we want her to join, and she can join if she goes through an initiation."

"What initiation?"

"We'll make it up. Hard stuff that she has to do—so hard that she won't be able to do it."

"It shouldn't be anything impossible," Jules said. "That's not fair. But it wouldn't be a bad idea to have

her do something that'll help the club get money, or
have her do something funny.''

"Yeah," Sam said. "Something funny. I'll be in charge
of initiations, okay?''

"I guess so," Jules said.

I felt a little annoyed that Sam was taking over, but
he was vice president and I was only treasurer. When
we came around the side of the house the new girl,
Betsy, was still sitting with Willie on the porch steps.
Sam pulled us down in the bushes so we could watch
and listen for a few minutes without being seen.
Through the leaves I caught a glimpse of frizzy hair. I
laughed and poked Sam.

"They aren't talking loud enough," Sam whispered,
as he yanked us both up. "Come on," he said. The
three of us came out of the bushes and approached the
steps.

"These are my friends," Sam said to Betsy. "We have
a club.''

"Greetings," Betsy said with a wide smile. I took a
good look at her face. She did wear glasses, but she
wasn't ugly. She might be a brain; you couldn't always
tell. Sibby, for instance, looked sort of brainy but was
really a moron.

"I'm Betsy Harris," she stood up. "I come from Syracuse, New York." She did sound different. Sam was
right about that.

"Want to join our club?" Sam asked. He was pretending to be very friendly.

"Who are they?" She nodded to Jules and me. Sam was no good at introducing people.

"I'm Jules. She's Ellis. We live back there." Jules pointed to Milford Square. "Our club's giving a magic show."

"It's a magic club?" Betsy joined us now, leaving Willie alone on the steps. She had probably already discovered what a baby he was.

"It's the Milford Square Good Citizens' Model Airplane Club," I told her, "but we do all kinds of things. Mostly we help the war effort."

"Want to join?" Sam prodded.

"I might. Are there any fees?"

"Fees?" The three of us exchanged glances. "You mean money for dues?" Jules asked.

"Or membership fees when you join?" Betsy gave him a direct look. She must have had a lot of experience belonging to clubs.

"Well, there *is* a membership fee," Sam started talking fast, "but there's mainly an initiation. If you don't pass the initiation you can't get in."

"What does the initiation include?"

"That's secret," Sam said. "You want to join or not?" He was rushing her, I thought.

"Well, you have to give me some clue about the initiation," Betsy said. She sure wasn't dumb.

"It's nothing bad," I told her.

"Who else is in the club?"

"The three of us," Sam began, "and . . ."

"The *four* of us . . ." Willie grunted from the steps.

Sam was impatient. ". . . and my sister, and Ellis' brother, and a kid named Tim and a girl named Sibby. Want to join?"

"Tell me what I have to do for the initiation, and I'll let you know."

"It's all secret. Come to the Milford Square mall," he pointed, "at two o'clock sharp. We'll tell you then what you gotta do."

"Okay," she agreed. "I'll ask Mama."

"Mama!" Sam snorted. "Where's 'Mama'?"

"In the house now, but she's leaving soon for the office."

"What office?"

"Her office. She's a lawyer."

"Oh, yeah?" Sam looked as if he didn't believe her. "Then where's your father?"

"He's in the Army," she said.

"Oh, yeah?" Sam looked at her in a slightly new way. His father was only an air raid warden. "What rank?" he asked.

"He's a captain and a doctor." Sam didn't have anything to say to that.

"Come on," he motioned for us to follow him. "Hey!" he called back to Betsy. "One more thing. The first part of the initiation is if you talk to anybody in the club before two o'clock you get paddled." He said it with a laugh, as if he expected her to make the mistake of answering right back. But Betsy didn't. She shook her blond head up and down to show Sam she understood. "And one *more* thing," he giggled, in a high voice, as she turned toward the house. "Say hello to 'Mama' for us!"

"She's not so bad," Jules said as we walked back through Feeney's yard. "What do you think, Ellis?"

I hadn't thought she was so bad, either, but I didn't like the idea that Jules was sticking up for some new girl. "Except for her frizzy hair, and funny accent and her 'Mama,' she's wonderful," I laughed. Jules gave me a surprised look.

"Yeah, I guess her hair does stick out," he said. That made me feel better. Suddenly I was really in the mood for teasing Betsy.

"What things are we going to make her do for the initiation?" I looked at Sam.

"I have a good one!" He grabbed Jules' shoulder and whispered in his ear. The two of them laughed.

"Tell me!" I said, but they only laughed louder. Boys were making me sick.

"No, I was just kidding around," Sam went on. "This is really it. Come here." We formed a huddle, and Sam whispered his plan. Even I agreed that it sounded pretty funny. I couldn't *wait* for the initiation to start.

T welve

About one thirty I sat leaning against a tree on the mall. Jules and Sam hadn't come out yet. I felt confused. On the side against Betsy, she *was* sort of different. It would be a big insult if Jules started hanging around with her instead of me. And who ever heard of calling your mother "Mama"? On the positive side, I knew that the way somebody's hair looked didn't matter much, she had stood up to Sam pretty well, and it might be very interesting to have a friend whose mother was a lawyer. After all, Nancy Drew only had a *father* who was a famous criminal lawyer. That was a lucky break, but it wasn't so special. Having a lawyer *mother* might really help a girl get into detective work. If I got to be friends with Betsy Harris maybe I would have a chance to get into that field. All of this, of course, would only be possible if Betsy was interested in being a girl detective. From our first meeting, though, I had a hunch that she might.

Jules and Sam, carrying a paper bag, came out of the McConagy's house just as a truck pulled into Milford

Square. I knew right away that it was Sibby being delivered by her father's handyman. I had telephoned earlier to let her know about the club initiation. Tim Feeney, Mick and Ruthie joined us on the mall.

"Where is she?" Sibby asked eagerly, before she had gotten out of the truck. "Where's the new girl?"

"She's supposed to come at two," I said.

"Poor her!" Sibby gloated. She loved having someone worse off than herself.

"What are we going to do to her?" Sibby wanted to know. But I didn't have time to answer. By the hedge around the Feeney's backyard I saw a frizzy head coming toward us. We all sat silently in a circle watching her. Behind Betsy trailed Willie Pflug. We had one hundred per cent attendance.

"The meeting will come to order," Jules said, when Betsy stood outside our circle. "Sam is vice president. He's in charge of initiation of new members. Now he'll take over." Jules sat down and Sam, with his paper bag in his hand, got up as if he were a dictator.

"Sit in the middle," he motioned to Betsy. "The first part we all do," he said. Sam dumped the bag out on the ground. At first I didn't recognize what was in it—it looked like a gooey porcupine. Looking closer, I saw that Sam had dug up soft tar from the street, rolled it into balls about the size of walnuts, and stuck each ball on the end of a stick. In the bag his tar "lollipops" had formed one big blob, with sticks coming out like porcupine needles.

"Special initiation lollipops," Sam said. He pulled

them apart and gave one to each member. "You can talk now," he told Betsy, but she shook her head and pointed to her watch. It must have been a couple of minutes before two, and Sam had said no talking until two.

"This is the first part of the meeting." Sam announced. "Everyone must lick a lollipop. Otherwise you're out of the club."

"Yuk!" Sibby made a face at the tar ball, but I winked at her to show that we were just going to pretend.

"These are delicious," Sam said. "A new kind of licorice invented during the war." He drew the lollipop close to his mouth and smacked his lips as if he were enjoying it. Jules, Sibby, Tim and I imitated him.

"Best thing I've tasted since watercress!" Sam shouted.

"I'm not doing it." Mick said. He got up, threw his lollipop on the ground and headed for the house.

"You sissy—you're out of the club!" I called after him.

"So what!" he said, slamming the door.

"Okay, Betsy." Sam stood over her, hands on his hips. "You gonna eat it or not?" Her tar lollipop, stuck all over with bits of leaves and fuzz, looked disgusting.

Betsy checked her watch before speaking. "Yum, yum!" she murmured, pretending to lick it as we had done.

"For *real*," Sam said. "Your tongue's gotta touch it."

Betsy touched her tongue to the tar.

"It has a delectable flavor!" She was a pretty good actress.

Sam smiled as if he was satisfied. "Willie, you too," he said. Willie gingerly put his tongue on the tar. If his mother had been there, she would have had a fit.

"Oh, my gosh, Sam," I said, "look at Ruthie!" While the rest of us had been faking, or brushing the tar against our lips, Ruthie had stuck the whole thing in her mouth. There was a ring of black around her lips, and she was chewing on the remains of the tar.

"Make her spit it out, Sam," I begged.

"Ruthie!" Sibby cried. "You're going to die!"

In the middle of all the screaming, Sam stayed calm. He raised his hands to quiet everyone down.

"It's true," he said quietly. "The people who *really* put the lollipops in their mouths are going to die. The rest of us were just pretending. The tar is poison."

Ruthie didn't care. She was still chewing the last piece of tar, even though I tried to force it out of her mouth. Betsy was snickering to herself. She seemed to think the whole thing was a good joke. But Willie Pflug was scared. His face turned pale, and his chin quivered.

"I'm going home," he said, starting to cry.

"Wait, no you don't," Sam stopped him. "We don't want your mother to see you like this." Sam sat him down on the ground. "Look," Sam said with pity in his voice. "It's affecting him already. He's got ear lobes. Did you ever notice that before, Jules?"

"No, I didn't," Jules said seriously. "Poor Willie's got ear lobes."

"And he's got tear ducts," said Betsy.

I wasn't sure what they were, but it was probably

something normal like ear lobes that just sounded bad. Sam and Sibby, who weren't very good at keeping a straight face, doubled over with giggling at Willy. I personally was still worrying about Ruthie, who had really eaten a blob of tar.

Willie sat sobbing with his head between his fat knees. "I'm gonna die," he wailed. "Let me go home!"

"No," Sam said, "we can't do that. The disease you get from the tar is catching. Everybody sit down! Because of this terrible thing that has happened—three kids eating poison, but mainly *two kids,* Ruthie and *Willie*—we're sending Betsy on the next part of her initiation." Everyone listened closely. Willie even choked back his tears for a second. "Betsy, you have to go up the hill to Windsor Avenue and knock on the door of the Gruen Funeral Home." Sibby gasped. "Tell them that two kids aren't long for this world, and you want Gruens to come down here in their black hearse and get 'em."

A scream from Willie started low and rose higher and higher. "Help!" he shouted, struggling to get away. But Sam sat on his legs and wouldn't let him up.

"Ellis," Sam ordered, "you and Sibby go with Betsy to make sure she does what she's supposed to do at Gruen's. Jules, Tim and I stay here to guard the victims. We can't have 'em spreading their disease around."

"Okay, Sam," I answered, "but for Pete's sake, get Ruthie to wash out her mouth." I was pretty nervous. I didn't think the tar could kill Ruthie, but I wasn't absolutely sure. And I wasn't looking forward to going to Gruen's Funeral Home. That place gave me the creeps. Sam always had to carry things too far. Maybe Sibby and I could start walking in that direction and then let Betsy off without doing her initiation test.

Sam, struggling on top of Willie, grunted to Jules, "Give Ellis your pencil and pad. Ellis, you write down what Betsy says at Gruen's." I saw that it would be hard to fake it.

At first the three of us walked silently up the hill toward the funeral home. I would have liked to just talk to Betsy, to find out whether she was interested in being a girl detective. But the club initiation and the orders from Sam made me act a little bossy.

"What am I supposed to say when we get there?" Betsy asked. She was taking the whole thing like a good sport.

"You're supposed to tell them that two kids on Milford Square aren't long for this world," I said. "Tell 'em to send the hearse. Sibby and I'll just stand on the corner while you go up to the door." I didn't want to go any closer than I had to.

"How will you write down what I say?"

"Don't worry, I'll hear."

The Gruen Funeral Home looked forlorn in the summer heat. The sun beat down on us as we stood on the corner waiting for Betsy. She made her way up the steps to the front door.

"What if there's a funeral going on right now?" Sibby asked. I didn't answer her. I planned to run if anyone came to the door at all.

Betsy rang the bell. "I wouldn't do that for a million dollars," I told Sibby. We waited. Then after a minute, the door was opened by a man in a dark suit. In spite of what I had planned, out of curiosity, I stayed rooted to the spot. Betsy stepped inside, and the door closed behind her. Sibby and I looked at each other.

"Ellis, what if she never comes out!" cried Sibby.

"Don't be a simp," I said, but I was thinking the same thing myself.

Though we had no watches, I saw the minutes ticking by on the big clock of the Windsor Hosiery Mills in the distance.

"What's taking her so long?" Sibby whined. I shook my head helplessly. The two of us sat down on the hot pavement.

"Let's go," Sibby said after another few minutes. "Who cares what happens to her. She's not our friend."

"We can't leave," I argued. "We were sent here to guard her. Let's pretend we're girl detectives." There was nothing I felt less like doing than sneaking up on Gruen's, but I figured that if I was really going to be a Nancy Drew I'd probably have to do much worse things. "Follow me," I said.

I crept up to the front porch without making any noise. Slowly I tiptoed up the steps with Sibby hanging behind me. At the front window I tried to peek in, but the venetian blinds were in my way.

"Around the back," I whispered. The back was spookier than the front. Shiny black cars were lined up by the garage. There were two entrances, one by the garage, and one through an enclosed porch. I was sure that the one by the garage led to where the bodies were kept. Inching my way along the side of the house, I went up the steps by the porch and leaned over to look in the window. Suddenly a face peered out at me, and the porch door creaked at my elbow and made me jump so hard that I knocked against Sibby and we both fell off the steps.

"Help!" I cried.

"What's the big deal?" said a voice. Betsy stood at the top of the steps laughing at us. "Good-bye," she waved to a man and woman inside the enclosed porch. "Thank you!" I recognized the woman as Marybeth Gruen's mother.

"What were you *doing* in there?" Sibby sputtered, as soon as we were out of earshot.

"They gave me lemonade," Betsy said. "They were very nice. That was Mrs. Gruen and a man who works for Mr. Gruen."

"What did you say at first?" I asked.

Betsy laughed. "Promise you won't tell the others?" I nodded. "Promise you'll put down what I tell you in the notebook?"

"Yes." I said.

"Okay, write down that I asked the man in the black suit to come down after Willie with the hearse, and that the man turned into a vampire and started chasing me, but I got away."

"Sam won't even believe it," I laughed. "What did you really say to that man?"

"I said, 'I'm new in Wissining, and I got lost. May I use your telephone?' "

"Did you use the phone?"

"Yes, but I knew no one would answer—Mama isn't home. Mrs. Gruen wanted to drive me around looking for my house. Wouldn't that have been something, to pull into Milford Square in the hearse?"

"Poor Willie," I said. "It's good you didn't let her drive you."

"When I saw your face at the window, I said to her, 'Oh, there's my friend. She'll show me the way home.' "

"Mrs. Gruen never knew it was a joke?"

"Nope," said Betsy. "She thought I was really lost. I can be very sneaky when I want to."

"Sneaky enough to be a detective?" I asked.

"Oh, sure," Betsy said. "I often do detective work."

"Do you read Nancy Drew?"

She gave me a look something like the looks I usually give Mick. "Nancy Drew is infantile," she said. "I *used* to read Nancy Drew. Now I read Judy Bolton mysteries. Want to see my Judy Bolton books?"

"Yeah!" This was turning out better than I thought.

"Why do you call your mother 'Mama'?" Sibby interrupted. She was probably annoyed that Betsy and I were talking about mystery stories and getting to be friends. " 'Mama' sounds like baby talk," Sibby sneered.

"Because 'Mother' sounds too formal, 'Mommy' sounds too ordinary, 'Mom' sounds too boyish, and French '*Maman*' sounds too affected. Besides Mama likes it, so it's good enough."

"Is your mother—your mama—by any chance a famous criminal lawyer?" I asked.

"No, she works for the government. But she knows a thing or two about criminal law."

"You're in our grade, aren't you?" I asked. Betsy nodded. "That's good," I said. "We can walk to school together in the fall, if you want."

When we reached the bottom of the hill, Betsy nudged me. "Get out the notebook. Try to fool Sam."

"Willie must have fainted by now," I said, as we turned into Milford Square. "Is he still screaming?"

The three of us looked toward the mall, but it was deserted.

"Hey, what happened to those dumbbells?" I looked around, half expecting Jules and Sam to jump out of the bushes. "Sam?" I yelled. Sam was sitting alone on his porch. When he saw us, he ran full speed across the mall and fell into step with us.

"She did it!" I grinned. "She went into Gruen's!" But Sam grabbed my elbow and made a sign for me to hush.

"Initiation's over," he said. There was something strange about his voice.

"Did Ruthie get sick from the tar?" I asked.

"No, Ruthie's okay." He stopped walking. "While you were gone a messenger came to Jules' house. Jules' mother got another telegram about Les," he said very softly.

T*hirteen*

That evening a strange quiet settled over Milford Square, and by the next day all of Wissining knew that Les had been killed in action. The War Department said they regretted to inform the McConagy's that the new list of war dead in the Pacific included Les' name. The Sunday morning edition of the *Windsor Times* printed the same picture they had run when Les went away. I cut it out and stuck it in my notebook at the place where my story about Les stopped.

In our house we spoke in hushed voices. My mother had been the one to tell me the news.

"Have you heard?" She had met me at the door when I had come in from the club initiation.

"Sam told me Mrs. McConagy got a telegram." I was breathing hard and my insides seemed to be melted, even worse than they felt while I was waiting for the results of the Citizenship Award.

"The news is bad," she said, twisting the edge of her apron. We stood in the dim hallway looking at each other. "Les is dead. He was killed in action on the island of Iwo Jima." My mother reached out to put her arm around my shoulder, but I pulled away.

"The dirty Japs!" I shouted, running to my room and slamming the door. I felt like smashing everything in the world made in Japan and Germany and any other countries that were Axis Powers. I waited by the door for a minute, half expecting my mother to follow me, but when she didn't I flung myself down on the bed. Though I had expected to cry, no tears came. "Cry!" I told myself. I just felt numb.

Then, while I was lying there, a lot of pictures went through my head, some real and some that I made up. Mrs. McConagy's face when she saw the telegram; Les hiding in a foxhole and a grenade exploding; Judy— Les' old girl friend—kissing the soldier on the Fourth of July; Mr. McConagy shaking his head sadly and not caring at all about who wanted iced tea for supper. The one person I couldn't picture was Jules. What was Jules doing and thinking? He hadn't cried in front of me since we were babies. Was he crying now? Would he stay in his house, or would he come out and play as usual? What would we say to each other the next time we met? I tried out different things to say, but they all sounded stupid.

At supper no one spoke except my mother asking if anyone wanted anything. Even Mickey understood that things weren't normal. I went to bed early, but I couldn't sleep. The spooky Snow White bookcase started haunting me again. Once, when I dropped off to sleep

for a second, I woke up suddenly, thinking that I saw
the flash of a hand grenade, but it was only a light from
outside reflecting off my Citizenship Award plaque.
During the night it seemed that Les was alive and had
come to present a flag to the school, but when I woke
up I realized it had only been a dream.

On Sunday the whole family went to church. Usually
in church I passed the time by drawing on the church
bulletin, but on this Sunday I sat absolutely still.
"Please make it not true about Les," I kept praying
over and over. But I knew that that was useless. You
were supposed to ask God to help you accept things as
they were, not to ask Him to make people come back
to life.

As soon as we drove into Milford Square after church
we saw the police car in front of the McConagy's house.
I figured it had something to do with the news about
Les. It wasn't until we pulled up in front of our house
that we noticed the bunch of people talking to Pat the
policeman and to Officer Sharky, the Chief of Police.

"What's all this on a Sunday morning?" my father
asked. The Shoppe's grown-up daughter leaned in the
car window.

"Jules McConagy has gone and run off," she said.
"As if that poor woman didn't have enough trouble!"
She nodded toward Mrs. McConagy, who was standing
next to the Chief of Police.

"Run off?" My father couldn't believe his ears any
more than I could.

"Run off," she repeated. "Took off early this morning, they think. Now why would he do that? That poor woman." She shook her head.

My father got out of the car. "Stay in here," he told Mick and me firmly. A peculiar soupy feeling spread all over me. My eyes blurred, and I felt as if I were dreaming again. Jules—run away? How could he? What for? I couldn't bear sitting in the hot car.

"Please let me get out!" I begged my mother.

"Daddy says to wait."

"Please, I'm going to be sick!" I pushed my way past Mickey, out of the car, and into the house. I ran straight to the bathroom, and when I heard my mother's footsteps on the stairs I locked the bathroom door. "I'm all right!" I called, but my voice sounded as if it belonged to someone else.

"Ellis, open the door."

"I'm all right. I'll be out in a minute." As her steps faded away, I ran to the window and raised it until I could see the McConagy's porch. Mr. and Mrs. McConagy, followed by Chief Sharky, were going into their house. Pat was talking quietly to the neighbors, who seemed to be breaking up and returning to their own homes.

Suddenly I started sobbing and sobbing. To make sure my mother wouldn't come running, I threw myself down on the bathroom floor and buried my head in a towel to muffle the sound. When my body stopped shaking I knelt by the bathtub with its funny claw feet and pressed my forehead against the cool edge.

"Ellis!" my mother called.

"I'm coming!" I answered. But I didn't move.

I must do something to help, I told myself. I must try to think why Jules would run away and where he would go. Why would Jules run away? Because he was upset and angry and sad. But that wouldn't be like him. He wouldn't purposely want to make his parents worry at such a bad time. He must know that running away wouldn't help matters, unless . . . unless Jules had gone someplace that he thought *would* help.

Maybe he had received a message about Les—not a real telegram, but one of the special, mysterious messages that only came to him. Was it possible that Jules had gotten a message about Les and that he hadn't believed what the government telegram said? Once in a while there were stories in the newspapers about the War Department's making a mistake. Just a month before, a soldier from Windsor had turned up when his family had thought he was dead. Jules had gone somewhere special, I was sure. He had gone because he had *had* to. But where? If it was far away there was nothing I could do. Well, for certain I couldn't be of any use sitting with my head pressed against the bathtub.

"Ellis!" my mother shouted again.

"I'm coming!" I unlocked the door and went downstairs.

My father was sitting in the living room with his jacket off and his hands on his knees.

"Ellis," he said, "can you tell me anything that will help the McConagy's find Jules?"

"How do they know he ran away?" I asked. "How do they know he didn't just go for a walk or something?"

"Mrs. McConagy heard him in the middle of the night, but his bed wasn't slept in. They think he may have taken some of his things, and they think he took his money." I remembered that Jules had had about five dollars saved up. "Now, Ellis," my father leaned forward, "can you think where Jules would go?"

I didn't know what to say. First of all, I really didn't know anything, but second, even if I thought of something I wasn't sure whether I should tell on Jules. I was absolutely positive that he must have had a good reason for doing what he was doing.

"I know where he *usually* goes," I said, "but I don't think he's at any of those places now."

"How much money did he have—do you have any idea?"

"About five dollars, I think."

"That's good," my father said, turning to my mother. "Five dollars won't get him far."

"Ellis, did he ever say anything to you about going away?" My mother looked as if she were about to start crying.

"No."

"When did you see him last?"

"Yesterday—early in the afternoon. We were having our club initiation, and Sam sent me and Sibby up the hill with the new girl. I didn't see him after that."

"Is there any reason you can think of why he would

run away? Would the shock of the telegram affect him like that, do you think?" my father asked. I thought about whether or not to mention Jules' messages, but I decided not to. No one else knew about them, and I had no proof that a message had made Jules leave.

"I don't know why he would run away," I said.

"Come outside and speak to Pat." My father took me by the elbow. "Tell him all the places you can think of where Jules usually goes."

Pat smiled at me as if things weren't so bad. "Where do you and that fella hang out?" he winked. "Got any secret hiding places?" He seemed to think Jules was nearby, in hiding because he was so upset about Les.

"Well, we go up to Windsor Avenue. The Mingus Magic Shop, the Rialto, the Wee Nut Shoppe."

"Any clubhouse?"

"No, but we play in the woods behind the pavilion at the playground." Naming that spot made me think again of the Fourth of July dance. "And we go to the creek, by the springhouse, where you found Mickey that day."

Pat nodded. "I've already looked down there," he said to my father. "Would he be likely to go near the mine hole?"

Pat's face had a strange expression, as if he wondered whether Jules would jump in on purpose.

"If he did," I said, "you wouldn't have to worry. He's a good swimmer."

"Tell me, is there any place outside of Wissining that Jules has ever talked about wanting to go to?"

"No," I said, "not that I can think of. Unless . . ."
suddenly I remembered our talk the day before. "Unless, the Windsor Fair . . . he wanted to go to the Windsor Fair to see Mingus."

"Mingus the magician—that's Charley Wertz . . ." Pat
seemed to be talking to himself. "Well, that's a lead,"
he said. "Thanks, Ellis. You're a good girl."

I didn't see what I had said or done that was so good.
In fact, I felt almost *bad* mentioning the Windsor Fair
because I was sure Jules hadn't gone there, and I felt
sorry when I thought about Pat and Chief Sharky wast-
ing their time running around the fairgrounds looking
for Jules and maybe calling Chas. Wertz over the loudspeaker. The last thing Jules would be doing on the
day after the telegram came would be enjoying himself
at a magic show.

"Come in the house now," my father said gently.
"Stay inside." He seemed to be trying to protect me.
Maybe he was afraid I might run away too.

When Sunday dinner was over, the afternoon dragged
on forever. My father went out to meet Chief Sharky.
Some of the men in the neighborhood had offered to
help in the search. I begged to be allowed to go, but my
father had said no. I sprawled out on the living room
rug to read the funnies, but nothing in them was funny,
and every time I head a sound I would jump up to look
out the window toward the McConagy's house. The
blinds were pulled shut at Jules'; there wasn't a breath
of air or a loud sound in all of Milford Square.

I thought of trying to see Sam, but his house looked

closed up. I couldn't imagine breaking the silence by calling "Yo," or even by ringing a doorbell. The radio was no help in getting my mind off things. On the program "One Man's Family" a grandfather with a quivering voice had a pile of children and grandchildren who had nothing but troubles, and the old man got stuck with all of them. In the background I could hear my mother talking to Grossie on the telephone, probably telling her about Les and Jules. I was going to ask to speak to Grossie, but the idea of talking to anybody seemed awful.

About four o'clock, just when I thought I would explode if there wasn't some news, I got the idea of going over to Betsy's house. If she was home I could at least ask to borrow one of her Judy Bolton mystery books. And maybe she could give me some advice about how to help Jules. Leaving the house without telling my mother, I walked through the back alley to Betsy's. When I first stepped into her yard it looked as if no one was at home. Then I saw Betsy's frizzy hair blending into the bushes beside her house. She was holding a Mason jar in one hand, and when she saw me she made a sign for me to be quiet. With a lunge forward, she came out of the bushes cursing to herself.

"Salutations," she said. "I missed the bloody thing."

"What?" I didn't know what she was talking about.

"Almost got a grass snake. I missed the bloody thing by an inch.

"Was it bloody?"

"No! That's a very bad swear word in England. Don't

use it there or you'll get your bloody mouth washed out with soap. Where've you been since yesterday? What was that telegram that came?"

"You don't know about it?"

"No."

"Well, Jules has run away from home."

"Jules? Because of the telegram?"

"In a way. Jules' brother Les was missing in action. We were all hoping he'd turn up safe, but that telegram yesterday said that Les was killed."

"How horrible." It was a strange time to notice such a thing, but I couldn't help hearing that Betsy had a special way of saying "horrible." That must have been the way they said it in Syracuse, New York. "And Jules ran away because of his grief?" she asked.

"I don't know. The grown-ups sound like they think he might be in danger—you know—trying to hurt himself because he's so shocked, but I don't believe that. He'll be very sad, sure, but I don't think he's in danger."

"Where could he have gone?"

"Search me," I said. "I haven't told anybody else this . . . but Jules sometimes thinks he gets messages, you know, feelings that things are going to happen."

"You mean E.S.P.—extrasensory perception?"

"I don't know if it's that or not. He said he got a feeling before Les was reported missing. And another time my brother was lost in the woods, and I think Jules got a feeling that day that if we climbed up over the pipe Mickey'd be okay. We did, and he was."

"You think Jules got a message about his brother?"

"That's the only thing I can imagine that would make him go off. He wouldn't just hide because he was sad. Can you think of anything I can do to help him?"

"I'd go around to places where he might have gone and look for clues. For instance, did he get money out of the bank? Did he take clothes along? Did he take food with him?"

"He took his five dollars, the police said. They haven't told any other information, though."

"Then you'll have to do your own detective work. Judy Bolton would make a list of possible places, and then she'd check them out. I'll help you make a list." She tossed her jar on the grass. "Forget the bloody grass snake!" she said.

I felt a little better when I walked back from Betsy's house with my checklist. Still, as I slammed the screen door, I held my breath wondering what might have turned up while I was gone. Though it was early, the sun had gone down and the house was dark.

"Daddy!" I shouted, but he didn't answer.

"He's not home yet, Ellis," my mother called from upstairs. "I'm going to give you supper now. We won't wait for him." The thought of the three of us sitting alone at the kitchen table, pretending to eat, made me depressed.

After supper Mickey and I were curled up on the floor next to the big radio listening to the "The Jack Benny Program" when I heard my father come in the door.

"No news," he said quickly, as the three of us came

running. "They're pretty sure he didn't buy a ticket on any bus or train out of town. But we've combed Wissining—he's not anywhere here." My father sank into a chair and passed a hand over his eyes. My mother and I looked at each other and then back at my father.

"If he's not found by noon tomorrow," he said, "they're going to drag the mine hole."

Fourteen

I could tell by my father's face at breakfast in the morning that everything was exactly the same. He excused himself quickly. "You stick close to home today, young lady," he said to me, as he went off to work. I didn't answer. I had decided, no matter what, to look for clues. It made me feel bad to pretend to obey, but there was no choice. I checked the newspaper—it was full of news about the war, but there was nothing at all about Jules.

As soon as my mother was busy running the vacuum cleaner and Mickey was playing upstairs, I took my checklist and half a loaf of bread and left the house. Betsy had offered to go with me, but I had told her I'd rather go alone. Going with someone would have made it like a game. This was no game. Number one on my list were stores where Jules might have bought something to eat. If he had left home without breakfast and had taken money with him, he might have stopped for food.

First I tried Priscilla's Candy Store by the library, but she said Jules hadn't been in. Next I walked up to

Van Horn's Bakery and the Wee Nut Shoppe. Neither owner knew Jules by name, so I had to describe him each time. It was all pretty useless, since in both places they ended up saying very cheerfully, "If he comes in we'll tell him you're looking for him!"

While I was up on Windsor Avenue traffic was stopped for a railroad train. It suddenly occurred to me —what if Jules had jumped on the couplings and had ridden the train out of town! They said he hadn't bought a ticket, but riding the train free would have been a lot smarter. If Jules had gone somewhere, maybe it was to Washington, D.C. It might make sense to go to Washington, if you wanted to check on a government telegram. I even asked a man at the Rialto Theater where the train was headed for. He told me he believed it was going to Baltimore. Well, that's it, I thought to myself. Baltimore's near Washington. That must be what Jules did.

For a while I was so sure about my Washington hunch that I almost gave up looking for clues. I don't know what kept me going. Circling around purposely to avoid the mine hole, I headed for the creek. I knew Pat had already searched around the springhouse, but I just felt like walking someplace peaceful. I could hardly believe that the people I passed on the way were going about their business as if everything was normal. When I walked down the path at the bridge grasshoppers were singing happily in the fields. I felt miserable. I sat down on the bank to take off my shoes and let the water ripple over my feet. I ate a piece of bread. It must have been getting pretty late in the morning, but I didn't care. Then I stood up, tied my shoes together by the laces, slung them over my shoulder and started to walk in the direction of the sewage pipe.

As I got close to the cement pipe I remembered the day when I had been so scared because Mick was lost. That same wave of weakness and fear came back to me now, as I stood near the spot where Jules had dropped his watercress. There was Jules' jar, in fact, overturned but unbroken.

I climbed the bank, clutching at roots and rocks as we had done when Jules was helping me look for Mick. Crickets hummed, the earth smelled rich and for a second I forgot how bad things were. At the mouth of the pipe I hoisted myself onto the cement shelf. With my back to the opening, I looked through the trees over creek, field and winding road below. And when I dared myself to turn around for a quick look into the dark interior, I saw Jules. He was lying in the gentle curve at the very beginning of the pipe—asleep.

"Holy moley!" I said under my breath. I stood like a statue for a second, until it really sank in that I had found him.

Jules' head was resting on his arm, and he had a corduroy jacket flung over him like a blanket. Next to him was a cloth sack tied to a stick. It looked as if he had studied the way hoboes carry their belongings. The only other thing I noticed was Les' high school yearbook, which lay at Jules' feet. I debated whether to wake him or to sit by until he woke himself. The thing that helped me decide was the picture in my mind of the police dragging the bottom of the mine hole. If I could get Jules to show himself before noon then maybe they wouldn't have to stir up that cold, black water.

"Jules," I whispered. "Yo, Jul-lee," I said very softly. He opened his eyes.

"Ellis . . . he's dead." Jules spoke in an even voice, as if he weren't even surprised to see me, and I realized that he was half dreaming.

"Jules, wake up." I touched his arm. He looked me full in the face, his eyes growing larger. Then he propped himself up on one elbow.

"Ellis," he smiled and sort of chuckled quietly. "Ellis, I don't know where I am. I'm half asleep."

"You're in the cement pipe. Jules, why did you run away?" He sat all the way up, blinked, and pushed back his hair.

"Oh. . . ." he groaned. "Now I remember."

"Jules, everybody's very worried. Why did you run away?"

"Wait a minute—let's get out of here," he said. "It smells like garbage." He picked up the yearbook and dragged the cloth bag and jacket behind him. I followed him out onto the shelf where we sat with our feet dangling over the edge. The sun shining through the leaves made speckles on Jules' face.

"How did you find me?" He was fully awake now.

"It was just plain luck. I *never* thought you'd be here. I made a list of places to look, and the pipe wasn't even on it. I just wandered here by accident. I thought I was seeing a ghost when I first saw you! Jules, *why did you run away?*"

He stayed quiet for a second. "Well, I may as well try to explain it to you, because nobody else'll know what I'm talking about. They'll get it all wrong."

"Go on."

"When you went away with Betsy at the initiation," Jules began, "Sam and I were still sitting on top of Willie Pflug. Then this motor scooter drove up to my house; 'Hey,' Sam yelled to me, 'who's that guy on your porch?' I saw that it was somebody in a uniform. I went tearing into my house. The messenger was just going away. My mother was holding a telegram and staring at it. She didn't even open it. I was . . . sort of embarrassed. I pretended I had to go upstairs, but when I got to the top, I hung my head over to hear what she would do next. I waited a minute, and then all I could hear was this awful low sobbing that didn't stop. My father wasn't home yet. I didn't know what to do. I went into my room and shut the door. I guessed what the telegram said." Jules cleared his throat.

"Then what?"

"When I was in my room, I got this *feeling*. It wasn't exactly a message. It was sort of like an *order*, something I *had* to do, even though I didn't know who was ordering me."

"What was the order?"

"It was strange. The order was, 'Find the tree that Les and Judy were sitting under in the yearbook picture.' "

"What for?"

"It was as if some message about Les would come to me there. As if I wouldn't be sure about Les until I got to the tree."

"Where is the tree?"

"I didn't know *where* it was—then. And I couldn't run out at that moment to look for it. My father came home, they showed me the telegram, they telephoned people, everything was terrible. And it got dark. I decided when I went to bed to go looking for the tree as soon as there was enough light to see outdoors."

"You should have left your mother a note."

"I didn't want anyone to come after me while I was looking."

"Did you find the tree?"

"Yes, finally. It's not far from the springhouse. But I didn't find it until this morning. That's why I stayed out all night. I looked all over yesterday."

"Didn't Pat or Chief Sharky see you?"

"Were they looking?"

"There's been a big search, Jules. Pat even told me he checked the springhouse."

"I didn't get there until this morning. I was all over the woods of Wissining yesterday, checking every tree. Pat must have passed right by me."

"How did you know which was the right one?"

"The shape. Look at the picture." He opened the yearbook to the photograph of Les and Judy. "Come on, follow me. I'll show you where it is. Take my jacket!"

I was anxious to get Jules to go home, but I figured

I'd better do what he wanted me to. He scurried down the bank as fast as he could go with the book under his arm and the stick over his shoulder. When we came to the creek bed, Jules led the way over mossy rocks to the field in front of the springhouse. Though I had never noticed it before, I saw now, almost immediately, the tree he meant. It was the one in the picture. Jules pulled up short at the base of it and sat down in its shade.

"This is it," he said.

I threw down his jacket, my shoes, and the bread, and knelt, looking at the tree. "What happened when you finally found it? Did you get a message?"

"No." Jules let out a long sigh. "I don't know what I was expecting. My hopes were all built up, so I thought maybe I'd hear a voice, or something. You know, in the Bible people are always hearing voices and seeing signs from God and stuff like that. But when I saw it, it was just a tree."

"It's a nice one, though," I said. The fork was low enough to make it a good climbing tree. I stuck my bare foot between the two main branches and hoisted myself up to the lowest limb.

Jules looked up at me through the leaves. "Then, when I didn't hear any voice," he went on, "I looked around for a written note, or something carved on it, or *anything* special."

Just as he was telling me about looking for signs, my eye hit on something amazing on the limb above me. "Jules!" I shouted. "Look at this!" He stared right at the spot, but he didn't move. He shook his head sadly.

"Jules!" I said, "it's L.M.—Les' initials, carved right here on the tree!"

"I know."

"Isn't that special? Isn't that a sign?"

"*I* carved them there, this morning," he said.

"Oh." At first I felt let down, but the more I thought about it, the more it seemed right. I didn't really like the idea of a mysterious sign. It was nice to know that the initials were there because Jules had carved them. "Then you don't believe in your messages anymore?" I asked him hesitantly.

Jules stood up and clasped his hands around a low branch. "I guess not." He thought about it. "Maybe I never did. Well, I guess I used to . . . when I was younger." We were both quiet for a minute.

"How come you carved the initials?" I asked.

"To make my own message. To remember Les."

"Now it's his tree," I said.

"In a way," he nodded. "But you can sit in it."

" 'Don't sit under the apple tree with anyone else but me,' " I smiled. I didn't mean anything special by it—I was just saying the words to the song.

" 'Till I come marching home.' " Jules added the last line to the song.

"Do you think Judy knows Les won't be coming home?" I wasn't sure if Jules felt like talking about Les, but it seemed as if he did.

"She must know by now. It was supposed to be in the paper. She won't care, though." He made a face.

"Why not?"

"I saw her with somebody else on the Fourth of July," he said.

"A soldier?"

"Yeah."

"Where did you see them?" I asked him.

"In the afternoon, fooling around at the swimming pool, and kissing in the woods just before the dance."

"Before the dance? Did it make you feel bad?"

"Yeah, I guess so." Jules looked at me for a second and then lowered his eyes.

"Hey, Jules," I asked him, "now that you found the tree, what're you going to do?"

He picked up his jacket. "Go marching home," he said.

Fifteen

Coming back from the creek, Jules and I agreed to pretend we had met on the street near Milford Square. Neither of us felt like explaining the whole business about the cement pipe and the tree. As we came into the square through Feeney's backyard, we saw Jules' father standing on their porch. Jules dropped his jacket and hobo pack and ran toward him. Mr. McConagy didn't usually show how he felt, but when he saw Jules he threw his arms around him and hugged him hard. The word that Jules was back got around the neighborhood fast.

"He felt sad and wanted to be alone," I explained to anybody who asked me. My mother wondered where I had been all morning, but in her relief at Jules' coming home, she didn't push me about it. The police called off the dragging of the mine hole.

Once Jules was safe and the first pain of Les' death passed, things settled down a little bit in Milford Square. The hot days of July flew by, while all the time the war was "winding down," as they said in the newspapers. The McConagy's changed the silk hanging in their window from one with a blue star to one with a gold star, and at the end of July they held a memorial service for Les. Lots of people in town came to the service—friends of Jules and his parents, teachers from the high school, and a few of Les' buddies in the army. Judy was there. The minister who spoke said that Les had given up his life for us but that he was still alive in our hearts and minds. He *was* alive in my mind, building model planes, and playing first base and sitting under the tree that now had his initials on it.

Even though it was a sad time because of Les, good things happened too. There was a feeling of closeness between people. The Milford Square Good Citizens' Model Airplane Club finally held a magic show, with all proceeds going in Les' name to a veterans' hospital. We even got a mention in the "Around Town" section of the *Windsor Times*. "Local magicians conjured up a substantial $17.95 yesterday as a contribution to the Brandywine Veterans' Hospital," the paper said. "The contribution will be made in the name of Leslie H. McConagy, killed in action on Iwo Jima, 1945." We never would have made so much money, except that Shoppe's grown-up daughter gave us ten whole dollars.

The members of the club stuck together pretty much through the summer. Jules and I stayed close friends. Even though we never mentioned it, there was a sort of secret bond between us after the day I found him in the pipe. Even Sam Goff stopped being so terrible. Maybe it was because he felt sorry about Les, or maybe it was because his stepmother was home now and could spend more time with him. Her defense plant had closed on account of the war winding down. As far as the rest of the club went, Tim Feeney helped his parents a lot in their victory garden, but when he wasn't busy, he hung around with us more than with the St. Agatha kids. Willie Pflug, Mick and Ruthie were always underfoot as usual. Sibby called me one day at the beginning of August to tell me that she wasn't going to see me much anymore. Her father was going to send her to a private school in Windsor in the fall. I pretended to be sad, but I was really relieved that I wouldn't have to keep putting up with her.

Another reason why I knew I wouldn't miss Sibby was because of Betsy. Betsy's moving to Wissining turned out to be the best thing that had happened all summer. Naturally she had passed the club initiation. Sam still teased her off and on about her Syracuse way of talking and about her "Mama," but she never let it bother her. He also tormented her when he found out she couldn't swim or ride a bicycle. But even Sam had to admit that Betsy could do a lot of other things well. She could do card tricks, draw pictures of people's faces that really looked like them, identify bugs and mount them on pins and talk very fast in Pig Latin. I saw right away that I had been stupid to worry about whether she was pretty or not. She *was* pretty in a way, when you got to know her. Jules liked her, I could tell, but he didn't love her.

In the early days of August the whole bunch of us would go to the swimming pool to try to teach Betsy how to float. "You're all horrible! Glub, glub . . ." she'd yell at us as we laughed and she sank. Afterward we'd buy Popsicles from McKinley, who parked his orange cart in front of the pool in the afternoons. In the evenings we'd play Capture the Flag and Spud on the mall until our parents called us in to bed.

On one of those evenings there was another dance at the playground. I made sure to point out to Betsy who Sally Cabeen was. Sally was there with the same Tarzan boy she had danced with on the Fourth of July, and Marybeth Gruen whispered to me during intermission that Tarzan and Sally were going steady. This time there wasn't any big rush to dance with Sally, either; in fact, Jules and Sam stayed outside and played Giant Step and hide-and-seek with Betsy and me during the whole thing.

On August 6 two serious things interrupted the calm of those summer days. The first one affected the whole world. The headlines in the newspaper said: "First Atomic Bomb Dropped on Japan." This was supposed to be good news for Americans because it meant that the Japanese wouldn't be able to hold out much longer against us. I felt mixed up. I certainly wanted us to win the war—I even wanted to get back at the enemy because of Les, but the idea of a bomb as powerful as 20,000 tons of TNT scared the wits out of me.

The second serious thing affected our family. Grossie went back into the hospital. "It won't be for long," my mother said. I wasn't sure what that meant.

"Can I get to see her again?"

"I'll let you know," my mother said. When I went to bed that evening I had a nightmare. I dreamed Mrs. Lane got angry at me and locked me up in my glass-covered bookcase.

During the next few days my mother went to visit Grossie as she had at the beginning of the summer. I was supposed to make lunch for Mick and drag him around with me wherever I went.

"Why doesn't Grossie come to our house on Fridays anymore?" Mick asked me.

"She's sick, dope," I said. I wasn't so much annoyed with him as I was with not knowing more about Grossie myself. "Anyway, ask Mom," I told him. It was easier for little kids to ask personal questions. That evening he asked her.

"Grossie's very sick," I heard my mother tell him, as she was tucking him in bed. Things always sounded more important at bedtime, as if God was listening.

In the other room I heard Mick ask, "When'll she come to our house?"

"I don't think Grossie will get well enough to come to our house anymore," my mother said in a strange voice. I buried my face in the pillow and kept it there until the pillow was soaked with tears. I had guessed for a while about Grossie, but until that moment I hadn't admitted it to myself.

"They've surrendered!" Sam jumped over the porch divider and banged on our front door. "Yo, Ell-lee . . . the Japanese've surrendered!"

I didn't know whether to believe him or not. That was exactly the same thing he'd said two days before, when it had turned out to be a joke. Jules joined him on the porch.

"It's true, Ellis," he shouted through the screen door. "Turn on your radio!" I opened the door for Sam and Jules as my father tuned in the living room radio. My mother and Mick came running, and the six of us stood in a semicircle with our hands behind our backs as if we were at a ceremony.

"We repeat," the radio blared, "President Truman has just officially announced the unconditional surrender of the Japanese." The six of us drowned out the announcer's voice. Jules and Sam jumped up and down hugging each other and dancing around the living room. Then Jules, Sam and I cheered while Mick banged on the piano. My father and my mother, even though she was tired from going to the hospital all the time, smiled and clapped in time to Mick's beat. We could hear the same commotion from other nearby houses.

"Spit, spit, right in the Führer's face!" Sam shouted.

"Off we go, into the wild, blue yonder!" sang Jules, as the six of us stomped out the front door and into the street where everyone was gathering.

"Ring all the doorbells!" Sam told Mick and Ruthie. "Tell everybody to come out!" The two of them scooted around to every house while I ran to get Betsy. By the time I got back, almost every neighbor in Milford Square was outside, on the porches or in the street. Jules' parents were a little quieter than some of the others, but I could see that they were really happy. Then, all at once, without anybody suggesting it, everyone moved onto the mall. People who usually never spoke to each other were chatting and laughing together.

"Look!" I cried. "I can't believe my eyes!" I tugged Jules' shirt sleeve. "*Mrs. Lukesh is on the mall!*"

"This is the happiest day of my life," Jules said.

Then all the fathers gave the kids money, and we went in a group to Priscilla's Candy Store for ice-cream cones. Each of us carried three or four cones with a piece of waxed paper over the top to protect them, and when we got back to Milford Square we handed them around. They were all squishy and melted, but nobody minded. The next two days were declared holidays, and we stayed outside as late as we wanted.

The war was over.

Nothing you could see changed overnight after the surrender, but the whole world seemed safe at last. On V-J Day, the official day of celebrating victory over Japan, Jules and I took a walk down by the creek to look at Les' tree. When I got home, there was a note for me from my mother, saying that she had been called to the hospital suddenly. I saw that the world would never be safe all the time for everybody.

During breakfast the next morning the telephone rang. My mother answered it, and when she came back to the table, her eyes told us the news first.

"Grossie's gone," she said. "She never regained consciousness. Uncle Frank will come for me in an hour or so." She sat for a second with her head lowered. Then she pushed back her cereal bowl, got up, and did what I thought at first was a strange thing. She went upstairs, and soon we could hear her moving heavy things around. When I got up from the table I climbed the stairs and saw that she was cleaning out closets. "Just something to keep me busy," she said to me quickly.

Going to my room, I closed the door, lay on my bed and stared at the mark on my ceiling. I didn't cry—I had already done that. After a minute I got up and took the blue poetry book off the shelf—the book of Mary Ellis' that Grossie had given me. I rubbed the leather cover with my thumb. Grossie must have known when she gave it to me that we might not see each other again. I flipped through it, reading the first lines of a lot of poems. I had a feeling, from looking at the book before, that there was one in particular I wanted to find. Then I saw it. It was a little hard to understand, but I thought I had it figured out.

The bustle in a house
The morning after death
Is solemnest of industries
Enacted upon earth, —

The sweeping up the heart,
And putting love away
We shall not want to use again
Until eternity.

That's what my mother was doing in the closets, I supposed—keeping busy to take her mind off sadness, bustling around, sweeping up the heart and putting love away—love for Grossie. Just as Jules had bustled around carving initials in the tree, where he put away his love for Les.

I stared at the poem, thinking what a hard time it was—the end of so many things. Some of those things were the hardest I'd ever faced, like the end of Les' life and now of Grossie's. But some endings were good, like the end of the war. And some were just *there*, like the end of the summer. It seemed that such a lot of time had passed since the trip to Sibby's, the Citizenship Award, and the Fourth of July. Before I knew it, though, school would be starting, and there would be all sorts of beginnings again.

Suddenly I felt the same thing my mother must have felt. I felt like sweeping, or running fast or swimming hard—anything to be busy. Just about the only thing you *could* do when you put away for a while your love for one person was to start loving other people more—and to keep yourself very busy.

I wasn't exactly sure what to get busy at, but I put the poetry book under my arm, and passing by the room where my mother was still moving around, I ran as hard as I could down the steps and out the back door toward Betsy's house.

Robin F. Brancato grew up in Wyomissing, Pennsylvania, a suburban town which provided inspiration for the setting of *Don't Sit Under The Apple Tree*. She majored in creative writing at the University of Pennsylvania and has been doing graduate work in English at Hunter College and the City College of New York.

For the past ten years, Robin Fidler Brancato has taught high school English and journalism in Hackensack, New Jersey. She lives in Teaneck, New Jersey, with her husband, John, and her two sons, Christopher and Gregory.